TALES

FROM THE

CHECKERBOARD CAFÉ

(Illustrated)

ABOUT BRAZOS RIVER PIE & RAILROAD PUBLISHING CO., INC.

Brazos River Pie & Railroad Publishing Co., Inc. is a for-profit company formed by Jo and Brian Pettyjohn, Teresa Pierce and Carolyn Flint. The company specializes in the publishing of writers who produce gently written short stories and rhymed poetry about life in the world's countryside. The company also seeks out unpublished writers whose talent is yet undiscovered.

---

518 South Liberty Street, Port Angeles, WA 98362

First published in the United States of America in 2001 by Brazos River Pie & Railroad Publishing Co., Inc. www.brazospie.com

---

ISBN 0-9711834-1-4

Manufactured in the United States of America
First Edition October 2001

TABLE OF CONTENTS

TABLE OF CONTENTS (Cont.)

ILLUSTRATIONS

ILLUSTRATIONS (Cont.)

THE RESCUE

DANIEL BOUCHER

Most of the vehicles Frank owned were the kind that had one foot in the grave. By administering a little love and tender care, he could usually resuscitate these mechanical invalids and get all four wheels, if not always the engines, planted once again on firm ground. Mind you, most of his mechanical menagerie were teetering on grave's edge, but he was determined that they would not fall in. Actually, if Frank had spent as much time on a regular job as he did working on his cars, he could have purchased a much better one. It was, however, the principal of the matter, not the economics.

His present vehicle was an older sedan with a penchant for burning equivalent amounts of oil and gasoline. The cloud of smoke billowing from around and under the hood could have been a matter of concern to the Environmental Protection Agency. The car had had, in its original state several decades ago, a beautiful gray velvet-like interior. It was still gray, but the velvet knap on exposed surfaces had long since disappeared. It looked as if Frank had skinned a fifteen-year old dog with the mange to use as his seat covers. The exterior had the look of what a modern Picasso might do if unleashed on a car. The predominant color-swirl was rust. Frank's friends were of the opinion that the pattern of the rust was simply the car's way of communicating a request for euthanasia. He felt that their meager attempts at humor at the expense of his mechanical friend were simply to be pitied.

One of the highlights of Frank's day was when his car not only started, but actually continued to run. He would break into a grin and the world would be his oyster for a while, usually a short while. Frank was experiencing one of those heady days, cruising to work when he noticed a gaggle of teenage girls waving signs, trying to entice passing motorists to get their cars washed. It wasn't that Frank liked driving a dirty car, he was simply aware that dirt and rust, at least as it pertained to his vehicle, had a fixative purpose. In short, he worried that washing it might damage its structural integrity, so he continued a few yards past the car wash site to a then-red traffic light. He was sleepy that morning, and the red light took a long time to change. He placed the car in "park" and actually dozed off for a moment.

Frank awoke to find himself being dragged from the car by a large man in a flannel shirt. In the confusion of the moment, he thought, "My God, I'm being carjacked in a car that can accelerate from zero to sixty in just under five minutes! This is truly a testament to the stupidity of criminals!" He lay quite still, thinking that if he feigned unconsciousness, the brute would leave him alone. Frank heard the teenage carwash girls screaming "Call 911!" He was grateful for their taking the risk of being involved in the crime but was worried that the police wouldn't get there in time to save him. The brute dragged Frank away from the car and dropped him on the pavement. The situation took a turn for the worse.

The car-wash girls, seemingly intent on getting a customer from whatever source, started to dump buckets of water on Frank's car. His thankfulness changed to outrage at their crass commercialism. He thought, "If they think I'm going to pay for this carwash, they are sadly mistaken!" That's about all the time Frank had to think, because the brute began trying to kiss him.

"That isn't the way we do things in Texas!"

Frank "came to" and yelped, struggling away before a lip lock could be established. Frank was stunned, and the brute, from the look on his face, was stunned, too. Frank informed him that he was not that kind of a guy and "That isn't the way we do things in Texas." The brute said to one of his confederates, "I think he is delirious, he thinks he's in Texas!"

Frank said, "I know we're not in Texas, but it's where I live!"

The police arrived and proceeded to sort things out. Apparently the brute, whose real name was Stan, thought that Frank's car was in imminent danger of burning with Frank in it. After everyone's voices lowered to a normal pitch, Frank informed them that the small fire was a visual indicator that the engine was actually running and that the smoke was simply a by-product of that indicator. He went on to explain that he had not made the screaming noise; it came from the rubber inner tube replacement for the broken fan belt.

Stan and his entourage departed in an embarrassed huff and the police, after laughing at Frank's water-soaked hulk, left, too. The interior now not only looked liked a skinned dog, it smelled like one, too. The water damage to the chassis of the car was severe and could not be repaired. The rust and dirt that had at one time held it together was nothing but a memory. Frank's expression was one of abject sorrow. Gone were the memories of estimating speed by how fast the pavement went by the hole in the floorboard. Never again would he check the thirty-pound test fishing twine holding the trunk lid shut. Gone was the challenge of pull ing the light switch just far enough to make it appear the brake lights worked. The Pennzoil stock Frank had invested in would be worthless.

Life can be cruel.

MY BROTHER AND THE WASP MAN

DAVID L. KIRKLAND

I might mention that my brother, Mike, never did meet the Wasp Man, not even once, and so you may wonder right off if this is a true story or just another windy. Such suspicion would be natural enough if you knew that I fancied myself to be reasonably expert at fishing. Hardly was ever born the fellow who has learned to enjoy that sport without being well-tutored along the way in the art of "stretching" fish in his later rememberings. The story about the Wasp Man needs no such artificially induced growing, however, so I'll just tell it the way you would have seen it had you been there yourself. The best way to warm you up and relax any doubts is to tell you first about my brother, Mike, for that is really the proper introduction.

He is my little brother, a full five years younger, which seemed a lot of years back when I was in the tenth grade. Perhaps you can envision him as he was then: dark haired, a bit chubby, ten years old, his dark eyes smiling and full of mischief. We were outside together one fine summer's day when I noticed Mike over by our mother's peonies; he seemed intent on some solitary activity and, for once, was not traipsing around behind me. I could see that his hands were cupped and closed one over the other to make a hollow ball. I stood there watching him, my curiosity growing. Gently, he'd shake his hands and then hold them to his ear. This seemed peculiar enough that I wandered a bit closer to get a better view, but it was still a mystery, and finally I just had to walk over and ask.

"Oh, I caught a bee," my little brother replied in a tone that made it seem the most ordinary thing in the world. "Shaking your hands makes 'em buzz," he explained. Well, I need no convincing at all that catching and shaking a bee would make it buzz. Actually, even without ever having tried it myself, I was still altogether sure of it! Somehow, this activity seemed—well, imprudent. I could not doubt that he was actually doing what he said, for just as I was thinking it must be a trick, Mike opened his hands and out flew a honeybee. Mike kindly offered to let me try it. I just as kindly declined. Being a fine big brother and surely wiser than a little fifth-grader could be, I suggested that he ought to stop it before he got stung. He only laughed, not at all dissuaded, saying there was nothing to it. Then, he proceeded to do it a few more times right before my still-skeptical eyes, even bringing his hands up near my ear to hear the buzzing sound for myself. Had I possessed enough good sense, that likely would have been the end of it.

Still, I could not watch this peculiar sport without being altogether intrigued. Nor could a big brother watch all that long and fail to be brave enough to follow where his little brother so fearlessly led. So, soon enough, I, too, was capturing honeybees to hear them buzz. Neither Mike nor I ever had a problem with this odd entertainment until the time he decided that what worked for the gentle little honeybee ought to work even better—a bigger buzz, you see—with the much larger bumblebees. It did work just fine, the first time or two, but then Mike caught more than a buzz from one of his irate captives, and one such failure was enough to make Mike limit his fun to honeybees. I have thought of this often in my adult years and have been mightily tempted to capture a honeybee again as I did when I was young. I know from crystal-clear memory that it would be safe, and I know that the sting of a honeybee is simply not all that painful. It is, however, surely a hard thing to do, to rely on memory against all caution, without the example of someone else right there to prove it all over again.

"...bringing his hands up near my ear to hear the buzzing sound."

This leads me directly to the stranger tale about the Wasp Man. I was grown and visiting my father at his farm. The meadows had been cut, and the hay had been raked and baled but not yet put away when I drove up to Dad's driveway. He was glad to see me and glad, as well, to have help with the work; soon the two of us were out in the field, loading the pickup and hauling the hay back to the barn. Once there, we'd buck the bales up to stack on the second floor level. The barn was unremarkable in any way, being quite an ordinary, two-story, country barn with milking stanchions and pens down below and the hayloft above. Not unexpectedly, along the rafters of the second floor level, there were paper wasps galore. You will know the sort of which I speak; the nests attach by a thin stem to some surface, looking something like an upside-down mushroom. The downward-facing part is open rather than enclosed, with the individual compartments where the wasp larvae live bearing a slight resemblance to a paper honeycomb. Wasps would sit on the nest to tend the larvae with comings and goings, and the air would fill with wasps if we moved too quickly or got too close. The rafters were simply loaded with nests! Some of the smaller nests would have but three or four wasps devoted to them, but the largest had as many as fifteen or twenty.

These wasps caused us no problem nor concern as we first began bringing in the hay bales, but at the beginning we were at the floor level and, thus, far from the rafters. That was not to continue, for as we piled each additional bale one upon the other, we came inevitably closer to the wasps. Normally, it would not have been a worry, paper wasps being nearly as mild-tempered as mud daubers and not at all like their ornery relatives, hornets, but as the day wore on, we got hotter and sweatier and more tired. Each bale we added took away that much more space. The earlier luxury of being on a firm wooden floor with plenty of room to swing the bales slowly eroded until we were bent over, balanced unsteadily on stacked hay, trying to work each succeeding bale into spaces ever more confined and ever closer to the rafters. Even intending those wasps no harm, it was altogether too easy to disturb them, just from working in such close proximity. As with my brother Mike and his honeybees years earlier, this getting closer and closer seemed—well—imprudent.

About the time this worry was becoming full-grown in my mind, we had to pause from our work, for we had a visitor. One of the local farmers had earlier inquired about the prospect of buying some hay, figuring we had a good mix of grass and clover cut at just the right time. He was hoping that Dad had some bales to spare. A bargain was quickly struck, and it was a good exchange, Dad more glad to have the extra money than he would have been with the extra hay. We had almost finished putting the hay up, not being sure the buyer would really come and needing to get it inside against the chance of rain. So, the sale of fifty bales meant that we'd need to start bucking the bales back down! It required no consultation between us to volunteer to allow the buyer to pick out his own bales. We stood ready to help, of course, but our unspoken thought was that we'd rather it was him—and not us—crawling inside rafter-high with his head up next to those wasps. Dad did cheerfully suggest that he might want to be a might careful, since we had packed the bales pretty close to the nests. The man smiled and shook his head.

"Those wasps are nothing," he said. "Come on in here a little closer, and I'll show you how to take care of them." Now, some country folks are not above playing a good joke, and his tone seemed altogether too nonchalant for me. I came along, just as he asked, but lingered close enough to the hayloft door so that I could leap out if the situation merited quick action. He went right up to a medium-sized nest, and spread his hands wide to either side. "You watchin'?" he asked. For sure, I was, with no idea what he might do, but a clear one of what I might do if he caused a commotion. Suddenly, he clapped his hands together, smashing flat the nest, wasps and all, instantly rolling his hands together, much as you might roll a large cigar. With a fine, big smile, he turned to exclaim, "Ah....got 'em all!" This was, even watching, simply unbelievable! He allowed as how it was no big shakes, that the secret was to add the rolling motion which kept the wasps from exacting revenge in their final moments. He asked if we'd like to try. We did not wish to try but did wish to see it again. Several times he repeated his performance, expressing disappointment if his timing was off enough that a single wasp managed to take flight before his big, calloused hands crashed together. Never once was he stung. I was amazed. Even Dad, with all his years of country living, professed never to have seen anything like this. Yes, we had absolute proof in those crumpled paper wasp nests littering the top of the hay bales where they had fallen. We knew it was possible. Did we try it? No, we did not. Even watching this repeatedly had not convinced us that it was possible to roll wasps about using one's bare hands.

After the fellow left, I told Dad how Mike and I had caught honeybees years earlier, this incident having brought back that memory. Dad just laughed as if it were a great story, which puzzled me until he explained. "You were lucky," Dad said, grinning widely, "that Mike was not here today." He was right, of course. Knowing us both, he was thinking that Mike would have surely given it a try when I declined, little brothers being ever little brothers and willing to try for bragging rights. What choice would I then have had? Why, just as surely I would then have had no real choice, the risk of stings, even all those years later, still being easier to bear than the indignity of failing to match my little brother's feats.

I have wondered, from time to time, about whether Mike still catches honeybees now that he has grown children of his own. My curiosity has drawn me to the telephone more than once, much as it drew me to him all those years ago when he was catching bees by mom's peonies, but I always remember in time the twinkle that still sometimes lights his eyes. I am not the only fisherman or storyteller in the family, you see, and I believe my asking had best wait until he can answer me by showing instead of telling!

THE FLEET SISTERS

SHARON LAFRENZ

Ignoring for the moment the unique psychological makeup of the two women, if the most notable physical characteristics of the Fleet Sisters, Deirdre and Cynthia, were to be combined, an unforgettable picture would emerge: the younger sister, Cynthia's, startling indigo glass eye would be most prominent. Her other eye was also blue, of course, but a more dour, grayish blue, the blue of a late winter sky hanging low over the comfortably secluded Purple Mountain Valley village of Skull Creek.

And then there was her sister, Deirdre's, extraordinary hair. The elder sister's ambitious and, some said, perfidious nature seemed to be evidenced by her stupendous flame-red mass of hair, which somehow wound itself into a remarkable halo of sorts.

As for their body types, the word svelte would probably not be heard in direct connection with either of the Fleet Sisters, one of whom won the Skull Creek Pizza Fest contest every single year, displaying vigorous appetites and titanium constitutions.

So a combination of the two sisters might present a solidly built, two-tone-blue-eyed, crimson-headed, angelic apparition of some wonder. There was, however, no mistaking the devilish Deirdre for a heavenly being: as most everyone in Skull Creek knew, she could have taught Satan himself a thing or two regarding the ancient art of iniquity. Few had proper respect for her powers of perdition.

Martin Amos, the postmaster of Skull Creek, was one who did. "She's a mean one," he'd tell anyone who'd listen. "Both of them Fleet sisters has always scared the skivvies off me, let me tell you. Even before Cynthia got that glass eye of hers, she had that creepy-crawly look, the way she'd get you in her sights and set that snake-like slit of a mouth of hers, daring you to say something –anything! You'd be better off not to!"

Martin's pink face would grow cherry red as he ranted about the evil sisters. His voice lowered when he honed in on the one he loved to hate the most.

"But scary as the younger one is," he'd say, "it was always Deirdre was the wickedest. Why, when they was but little scamps, that Deirdre – the oldest one – she already had a terrible.....whaddayacallit.....aura about her. It was like a mist a' malice, that's what, kinda like floatin' all around her. Bet you don't know how it came about that Cynthia's only sporting one eye, do you? Mind my words, if you value all your working parts, don't get in that flaming-haired Deirdre's way! You'd do well to steer clear of both of them. Them two, they're the combo from hell."

Another distinct characteristic of this combo from hell would have been Cynthia's whine, which to Martin Amos was a torturous companion to her amphibious glare. "That woman has no voice," he declared, "only a screechy, high-pitched whine you'll wish you never heard if she decides to treat you to it. Could be that witchy Deirdre had something to do with that, too; I don't know. Cynthia was whining long before she acquired that glass eye. Not when she was a kid, though. No, I remember when she actually sounded human. Too bad she didn't just take up sign language after she lost her human voice. I swear, I'd rather listen to a Siamese cat in heat twenty-four/seven than to be forced into a conversation with that one-eyed blood curdler, Cynthia Fleet."

Everyone in Skull Creek knew that Martin Amos had once been hip-deep in love with Cynthia. It was a long time back; but Martin, poor fellow, had been spurned. Not by Cynthia, but by her sister, who made all the decisions regarding the two of them. Two decades later he was still bad mouthing the Fleet sisters every chance he got.

Considering Martin's abhorrence of both sisters, all of Skull Creek was astounded when it was announced that Cynthia Fleet was about to become Cynthia Amos. Everyone wondered what in the world had possessed Martin Amos to propose marriage to a woman he'd now cross the street to avoid. No one planned to miss that wedding.

It had rained for days on end when suddenly, on the morning of the wedding, sunshine burst out of the sky and drenched all of Skull Creek with a glorious golden warmth. By noon, the muddy mess had dried up, and the perky little heads of daffodils smiled all over town. Everyone, including the new minister who would be performing the ceremony, saw this as a benevolent sign.

Inside the chapel, Martin Amos stood cool as a cranberry spritz at the front, decked out in a size-too-large rented white tux, pant cuffs flopping down over his white loafers, a red carnation tucked into his lapel. Long strands of silvery hair were plastered across the top of his shiny pink skull. Loose as a Slinky, hands clasped behind him, he appeared not at all nervous, as though he might be waiting on his peanut butter parfait at the Dairy Queen.

All heads turned in the packed chapel as the organ music announced the maid of honor. As Deirdre began her walk down the aisle, a collective gasp was heard. Wearing a floor-length fire engine red gown, the extraordinarily full skirt grazing the pews on either side of the aisle as she passed, Deirdre, head held high, gazed directly towards her about-to-be brother-in-law, Martin Amos. A circle of multi-colored flowers crowned her head, her fiery hair fanned out across her broad, creamy shoulders. Clutched close to her middle, she carried a matching bouquet. Regal? Stunning? Well, certainly unforgettable, the guests would all concur.

The bride came next, a cool cloud of white, on her own, stepping carefully down the aisle: step, pause..step, pause..step, pause. Cynthia's eyes, the dark blue one and the light blue one, were also aimed straight at Martin, whose narrow face was still blank as a boiled egg. In fact, the assembled guests noted, Martin seemed to be oblivious to what was happening.

But then, just as Cynthia stepped to her place beside him, Martin Amos broke into a grin like a six-year-old on Christmas morning. Oh yes, he knew what was taking place. And Cynthia, who hadn't been known to smile in decades, actually giggled a soprano lilt that was music to Martin's eager ears. Deirdre, the witchy woman herself, began to chuckle. Then the Fleet sisters began to laugh out loud, holding their bellies and wiping their eyes!

"Deirdre Fleet wasn't at all the wicked creature everyone thought she was"

Martin was breaking up, and the minister! Mirth set aside suspicion and spread through the congregation like Skull Creek gossip. Soon the guffaws were reverberating off the walls, shaking the stained glass windows, and dispensing a shower of joy on all those present. It was spontaneous convulsion, affecting one and all.

With great effort, the minister was first to regain his composure. "Dearly beloved," he began, smiling hugely, but containing himself. "We are gathered here...to witness the power of love. Can there be any doubt?"

He snuck a quick glance at the maid of honor. Deirdre Fleet glanced back. And she smiled at him. And the minister smiled at her, thinking to himself that Deirdre Fleet wasn't at all the wicked creature everyone thought she was. Heavens, no. Why, she was a vessel of love; love for her sister, who would now have Martin; and love for the one who was joining them in holy matrimony.

Wickedness, schmickedness— all it takes is love.

THE LEGEND OF LEEPER HOLLER

NORMAN MCFADDEN

Tenty D. Hation were an ol' one-armed man thet lived up at the end of Leeper holler. He were a wino and the town people didn't like him much. They would go the other way so they wouldn't have to see 'im or talk to 'im. Some of the kids liked ol' Tenty, though, cause he were a good storyteller, specially 'bout ghosts and other unearthly terrors in the dark.

Tenty woke up one mornin' an' sed to hisself, "I think I'll jes go and see if I kin ketch some fishes fer dinner." So Tenty dug some worms out by the outhouse and off he went. As he wuz walkin' down the holler, he saw ol' Doc Hurley's house. Doc was aworkin' on his picket fence an' sweatin' an' cussin'. So Tenty sed, "Doc, I'm goin' to the Meal Pond to git some fishes fer dinner. You wanna come?"

Doc got his jug of moonshine, the most important item of 'quipment fer fishin', an' his fishin' tackle. Doc asked Tenty what he had to drink and Tenty sed, "Nuthin', but we'll stop by Judge Luckily's store to borry his boat an' I'll git somethin' thar."

They walked down the road to Judge Luckily's store and Doc sed, "Why we goin' to the Meal Pond? I heered some turrible stories 'bout the monster thar."

Tenty laughed an' sed, "Thar ain't no monster thar! It's just a kinda scary lookin' place an' people's 'maginations get the best of 'em."

Judge Luckily let Tenty an' Doc borry his boat, but he sed, "Y'all be keerful of the Legend of Leeper Holler! I doan want my boat comin' back with teeth marks on it."

Doc looked worried an' sed, "What you mean, teeth marks?"

Judge Luckily sed, "Aw, you probly doan need to worry nuthin' 'bout the boat, thet monster ain't gonna eat nuthin' aluminum!" That didn't comfort Doc too much. He wuz thinkin' thet if the monster didn't eat the boat, there wuz only two other things on the menu...him an' Tenty.

Tenty sed, "Judge, give me a bottle of Annie Green Springs an' quit tryin' to make Doc afeered of the Meal Pond. Thar ain't no monsters in Leeper Holler."

Judge Luckily sed, "'Course, I doan know nuthin' fer sure, I jis know whut I heered. Thar's somethin' big an' turrible strong in the Meal Pond. Y'all be keerful!"

They walked on toward the pond carryin' all their stuff in the boat. Tenty wuz whistlin' an' Doc wuzn't sayin' nuthin'. He wus just shakin' his head back and forth and moanin'. Tenty listened to this fer a while an' sed, "Doc what's all the shakin' an' moanin' 'bout?"

Doc sed, "Tenty, there's stories I heered, too, 'bout something turrible big an' strong in the Meal Pond, an' now thet I think of it, I doan like the name of thet pond much either."

Tenty looked at 'im like you look at a kid who's afeered of the dark. "Doc, thar ain't no such things as monsters! The reason we're goin' to the Meal Pond is 'cause everbody else is afeered to fish there. If thar ain't nobody fishin' there, what do you think thet means? I figure the pond is chuck full of fishes!"

Doc looked doubtful. He thought about what Tenty said fer a little while, then he started noddin' an' moanin' agin. Tenty was gettin' expirated.

"Doc, what the hell you moanin' an' noddin' agin fer?"

Doc looked afeered an' sed, "What if the monster done et all the fish? What if, now thet he done et all the fish, he's powerful hungry fer sump'n else?"

Tenty sed, "Fer the last time, Doc, thar ain't no such things as Monsters! Whut people is talkin' about is probably a giant catfish, what's been livin' thar fer years 'cause nobody fishes the pond."

They got to the Meal Pond and looked out over the water. It was about two acres of prime fishin hole. All along the fur side wuz big hickory nut trees and some red cedars, growin' right on the bank. The hickory nut trees wuz hangin' out over the water. In the fall they dropped their hickory nuts in the water and made it coal-tar black.

Tenty and Doc wuz tired from carryin' the boat and sat down to have a drink. After two good swigs of moonshine, Doc began to feel better about fishin'. Tenty was layin' back on the grass and tiltin' his Annie Green Springs straight up. His Adams apple went up and down like thar wuz a frog in his throat. Sounded a little like thar wuz one in thar, too.

Tenty sed, "Let's put the boat in the water, it's gonna get dark and we want to ketch a mess a' fishes 'fore it gets too dark to see." So they slid the boat in the water, piled in and pushed away from the bank. They fished fer 'bout an hour an' didn't ketch nuthin'.

Doc begun to look over at the bank where the hickory nut trees wuz an' sed, "Did you hear that!?" Tenty looked over there, but he didn't see or hear nuthin'. They both sat stock still in the boat. The wind was comin' up a little an' the trees wuz startin' to make little shiverin' noises in the breeze. Tenty stood up in the back of the boat to git a better look at the dark bank.

'Bout that time a screech-owl let loose in the hickory nut trees an' Tenty sed, "Good God A-mighty!" an' fell down behind the back seat of the boat with his feet stickin' up in the air.

Doc sed, "Tenty, this place is givin' me the creeps. Let's git the hell outa here!" He was holdin' onto both sides of the boat, tryin' to keep Tenty from dumpin' them into the Meal Pond with the monster.

Tenty got back on the seat and sed, "Let's jes fish a little more. Thet wuz jes' a screech-owl. I jes' didn't 'spect it nohow." Doc looked at the dark bank an' didn't say nuthin'.

'Bout that time Tenty grabbed for his pole an' sed, "Man alive! I dun got a big one! Look at the way my pole's bendin'!"

"Damn, this thing is strong!"

Doc sed, "Can I hep ya? You sure you kin get it with jes one arm?" He wuz hafway in the back of the boat, tryin' to hep Tenty.

Tenty sed, "I'm stronger with one arm than most people is with two. Damn, this thing is strong!"

The more Tenty would pull, the more the thing in the water would pull back. Doc had a big chugalug of moonshine, all the while peering over the side of the boat—tryin' to see what Tenty had on his line.

All at once the boat began to move over to the hickory nut trees. Tenty was holdin on with all his strength. Doc was sayin' prayers for God to save them from the monster. 'Tween verses, he chugalugged some moonshine.

The boat began to go in circles and Tenty began to pray, too, 'cept 'tween his verses he chugged Annie Green Springs. Tenty wuz holdin' his pole under his right arm stump and the side of the boat with his left hand.

Doc sed, "Let the damned thing go before it kills us and eats us!" Doc wuz serious afeered an' if it hadn't been for the monster in the water, he woulda been outa thet boat.

Tenty sed, "You bein' a fool, Doc! We done caught the biggest catfish ever and we gonna have a fine dinner."

Bout thet time, the monster got to the dark bank and crawled out. It was as big as a pig an' hairy as a wolf! It had a horn right 'tween its eyes and it let off a cry thet sounded like a woman bein' hurt bad. It sent chills right through Tenty an' Doc. Tenty dropped his pole an' grabbed an oar. Doc grabbed his an' they rowed like crazy men back to where they went into the Pond. Doc jumped outa the boat and commenced runnin'. Tenty sed, "Wait a minit, Doc, we gotta take Judge Luckily's boat back!"

Doc kept runnin' an' yelled back over his shoulder, "The hell we do! We kin git it in the mornin'." Tenty ran after him. They got back to Judge Luckily's store an' told him what happened. Judge Luckily looked real close at 'em and smiled. Then, he asked how much of their wine and moonshine they still had.

They didn't go fishin' at the Meal Pond agin.

"...the monster got to the dark bank and crawled out."

HORSE SENSE

PHYLLIS MILETICH

It had been a long time since Fritz owned a horse. When he moved away from the old place, there were only two left and—as everyone does—one of them got old and just leaned into death standing on his feet. The other was pastured out away from the house, so Fritz couldn't see him and talk to him and civilize him. "You got to talk to a horse; otherwise, they get nervous and jumpy and lonesome, just like people do," Fritz declared.

Now, at seventy-eight, Fritz didn't pack professionally anymore; neighbors said he was making a career out of horse buying. He read the ads every night and, if anything looked tempting, he'd spend part of the next day checking it out. For the best part of the year, he was all over the county looking at horses, but nothing was "right." He had something special in mind, but nobody knew what.

"So they said it was an Appaloosa," he lamented to his wife, one night, "and you shoulda seen him! Damned old rattailed bugger, with them wild white eyes!" Nothing seemed to make it with Fritz. "And this one guy says he's got a good horse. Old hound-bellied, dish-faced damn thing, I wouldn't give him nuthin' for that horse. No wonder he's rich; he's tighter than the bark on a tree, anyway..."

And then one night, in answer to an ad, Fritz went looking again. "I went out to that pasture," he told a friend in wonder, "and there stood my horse!" Sonny, a big buckskin gelding, looked back at him calmly. It was love at first sight.

Now, as one might suspect, Fritz prided himself on being a good judge of horseflesh, and he was always curious to learn more. He had a young veterinarian friend—a round-faced, stocky man with a natural sense of humor. The "Doc" came over one day to find Fritz doing a rough autopsy on a horse that had died mysteriously. Not too delicate, but effective—he was doing the job with an ax.

"What happened to that horse?" the vet said in awe.

"I dunno," said Fritz, carving away. "A couple of days ago, he had the heaves."

"The heaves!" the college-trained vet sputtered. "Ah, come on now, Fritz."

"Listen," Fritz said to the kid, "there's a lots of things I don't know, but I know somethin' about horses." Then, remembering the Doc's college degree, Fritz threw in the final evidence: "I got books, too."

"Then, let's see them," said the stocky vet, and with that Fritz stopped his work and disappeared into the house momentarily. Bringing out a well-fingered, leather-bound gold printed volume, he placed it in the young man's hands. "Well, hell, Fritz," said the vet, "these books were written in 1916! They're no good now."

"Why not?" Fritz said with incontrovertible logic. "Horses haven't changed any since then, have they?"

Through the years an easy friendship had grown between the crusty old packer and the cityeducated young man. Sometimes it took the form of oneupmanship, for both men liked a laugh. Now, with his prize Sonny, Fritz went over to see the Doc for an appraisal. He dismounted just as the vet came out of the house.

Hands behind his back, the vet squinted into the horse's eyes. "What did you buy a blind horse for?" he demanded of the seasoned packer. "Don't you know better than that?"

Fritz smiled, "He ain't blind," he said with finality.

"Well, he's got a rupture, anyway," the Doc persisted, moving down to the horse's belly. "That's a rupture pokin' out there, ain't it?"

Fritz chuckled to himself. "He's a gelding, ya damn fool," he said.

The vet continued his circle around the stolid Sonny, hands still behind his back in the manner of a fair judge, sniffing skeptically. "Well, he's got the ring-bone and the spavins—that's for sure," he looked at Fritz triumphantly. "I think you got stung, Fritz. I thought you knew horses..." He moved around the other side of Sonny and stopped squarely in front of the animal again.

Throwing his hands in the air with feigned shock, he then slapped them over his eyes. "Well, my God, no wonder," he finished," his eyes round with wonder. "His damn chest's so narrow that both of his front legs are comin' out of the same hole!"

With that, Fritz pulled the last cinch on the saddle and mounted his prize majestically. He tugged at the brim of his red hat, grinned down at the young man, and rode off on the even-gaited buckskin. Now he knew he'd got a good deal. The Doc smiled easily after his old friend. "Hey, Fritz," he called after the retreating figure, why don't you stop over tonight for a while?"

"Well, is there gonna be any drinkin?" Fritz called back through the fading light

"Maybe," said the vet. "Why?"

"'Cause if there is," yelled the old packer, as he rode through the thickening trees, "I wanna know, so I can start practicing..."

And he disappeared though the woods, riding easily, as though heading for the mountains again, after all those years.

"...he disappeared though the woods, riding easily..."

THE PURGATORY SPEEDWAY

DAMIEN PADRAIC O'KEEFFE

The ranch that their father had told them about couldn't be the same place they were looking at! Paul had grown up a city boy. His father had regaled him and his eleven-year-old sister with tales of unimaginably exciting adventure on Windstone, the family ranch near Purgatory. Of course, these adventures had occurred thirty years before when Windstone was a working ranch. Gone were the hands who told stories around the campfire. Gone was Lupita whose tortillas tantalized their father's palate. Now, the ranch was a weekend retreat for their grandfather, an escape from his workaday world.

In Paul's eighth year, he and Pam had an opportunity to spend several days there while their grandfather stored hay for the winter's feed. The idea of spending some vacation days at a real ranch had seemed full of promise.

Their grandfather, and Paul's namesake, Paul Henry Tomlinson, was a man from the last century, or more accurately, the century before last. Mr. Tomlinson ("Grandfather," as they were required to call him) grew up on the ranch and had spent his youth herding cattle, digging postholes and clearing mesquite thickets for pasturage. Because the family had little money to spend frivolously during the genesis of the ranch, his idea of a "fun" day came to be one on which he did not have to dig postholes or clear mesquite thickets. As a result, he had little patience with easily bored children and even less experience at entertaining them. Nevertheless, he loved his grandchildren and silently promised himself to make their days entertaining.

The ranch had seen better years. Much better. Since the main herd had been sold off, no one had lived there full time. The buildings and fences reflected the lack of care that absence brings. The house's paint was peeling, several shutters hung at odd angles, the gate to the garden was attached by only one hinge, and the gray, unpainted barn's roof line was exhibiting a pronounced sag. The prairie Johnson grass which had grown high and reclaimed the pasture was beginning to encroach on what was the yard. To say that Paul and Pam were disappointed at the sight of this supposed playground of yesteryear would be to indulge in gross understatement. They saw no sign of anything they thought had the remotest possibility of entertainment value. Mouths agape, they were horrified. The reaction did not go unnoticed. Their grandfather realized that he might have his hands full keeping them entertained, or at least busily occupied.

He watched carefully as their television-trained minds grew quickly bored with the slow pace of entertainment at the ranch. The buckboard rides, the walks to the old Caddo Indian village site and the stories of his boyhood at the ranch occupied them for little over a day. It seemed that they were looking for something which could be consummated in less than thirty minutes. They looked at the cattle, looked at the horses, chased the chickens, threw stones into the algae-clogged stock pond, looked for arrowheads and petrified rocks and then settled into sitting on the ranch's porch swing, looking morosely at the windmill turning slowly in the West Texas breeze. Their boredom was such that they actually resorted to having conversations with each other.

Their grandfather was working hard, getting the hay into the barn for the winter. It was not the kind of job that inexperienced, young children should be around, so Paul and Pam were banished to the then-unoccupied house. Their grandfather broke for lunch on the third day, having loaded most of the hay into the loft a half-day ahead of schedule. "Grandfather, can we go to Purgatory and get a coke?" Pam whined.

"Yeah, I'm thirsty, and the water here tastes awful!" chimed in Paul. He was right. The water from the well was incredibly hard and had a taste that only a man dying of thirst could appreciate.

"I'm beat, kids," said their grandfather. "I have to take a little rest for a few minutes." With that, he lay in the shade of the porch and closed his eyes. Paul and Pam looked at each other in disappointment and frustration but said nothing for a few moments.

"Grandfather, what's that 'wing-lookin' thing stickin' out of the grass by the windmill?"

"Huh?" said their grandfather, without opening his eyes. "Oh, that's part of an old go-kart made from a Volkswagen. It hasn't run in years."

"Well, Grandfather, it has big, fat tires on it and a steering wheel! Can't you make it start?" Paul and Pam were showing signs of interest and excitement.

There was little reaction from their grandfather. He opened his eyes, briefly, but remained lying in the porch's shade. "The Cole family left that thing here. They raced them but blew the engine in that one." He closed his eyes again.

A competition go-kart, what a find! Paul and Pam raced out to the kart to examine it more closely. They brought brooms, cloths and a pail of water and began cleaning the years of dust and mud from the chassis. After about three hours, their progress was beginning to be limited by the Law of Diminishing Returns. Their grandfather was grateful and relieved that they were excited about anything and out of his way. He quickly completed the loading of the hay bales into the barn and drove his pickup over to the kart reclamation site.

"Hey, you kids actually have that old thing looking pretty good," he said. And smiling, "How would you like to wash my pickup?" Their faces reflected an emphatic disdain for the job, so their grandfather dropped the subject. "Go inside and put all those rags and brooms away." When they returned, they were surprised when their grandfather tossed Paul an old motorcycle helmet. "You ready to go for a ride, son?" Paul was thrilled. He assumed that his grandfather had repaired the go-kart. Then, he noticed the long length of rope extending from the front of the go-kart to the rear bumper of the pickup. "Be sure the helmet is on, Paul. You need to get something for your eyes, too!" Paul and Pam looked at each other a moment. She opened her purse with a mischievous smile and withdrew a pair of very large-lens, pink, very feminine, vintage Elton John sunglasses and handed them to Paul. He looked at them with distaste but having no alternative, took them anyway and mounted the go-kart. Their grandfather glanced at the apparition in his rear-view mirror and began to chuckle. Paul didn't witness his grandfather's mirth; he was busy getting ready for the adventure of his life. Pam climbed into the bed of the pickup, the better to witness the spectacle.

The pickup pulled the go-kart easily. Their grandfather kept the speed at about ten miles per hour and traced a wide circle around the pasture. Though the go-kart's tough ride made holding on difficult, Paul was enjoying himself immensely, hallooing as he and the go-kart flew into the air over bumps.

"Go a little faster on the way back, Grandfather," said Paul, meaning four to five miles per hour faster. Their grandfather floored the pickup, tearing down the road like a spooked steer. The problem of the go-kart's initially facing the wrong direction was solved when the speeding pickup took up the slack in the rope, and the go-kart did a mid-air 180 without requiring any input from its driver. Paul was slammed firmly into the seat which creaked menacingly. He noticed briefly the amusement the situation delivered to Pam but had little time to consider it. The go-kart's speedometer was registering forty-five miles per hour, and any comfort that the driver's chair had previously provided vanished. Paul's knuckles were turning white with the exertion of holding on when he noticed the pickup's brake lights come on. Paul slammed his foot on the brake pedal. It went all the way to the floor. No brakes! The only thing to do was to steer around the now-stopped pickup.

Their grandfather's face was a mask of suprise and concern as the go-kart, with Paul hanging on, shot by the pickup. When the go-kart reached the end of the rope it executed another unassisted, mid-air 180. This time, Paul

"...the go-kart, with Paul hanging on, shot by the pickup."

was thrown clear, landing in a large patch of Texas sand-burrs. He remained there, lying quite still, the shock of his experience washing over him. Their grandfather raced to him, picked him up, and asked if he was OK. He was eight and, therefore, indestructible and felt that he had joined that select fraternity of the family's males who had experienced true adventure at Windstone. He said he was fine. Pam was laughing uproariously and making disparaging remarks about Paul's driving talent, or lack of it. The sting of that criticism was softened when their grandfather threw her the battered helmet and said, "Your turn!" He started the pickup and began the trip back to the ranch house. Paul was in the pickup's bed, watching the expression of abject terror on his sister's face as she bounced along the pasture. He smiled.

Life was good in Texas that day.

MULE EGGS

DAVE PETITJEAN

Gettin' rich can be a wonderful thing! Some people get there through blind luck, others through inheritance, which is 'nother kind of luck. Most of the people who make it however, are there because of talent and effort. When you don't have the former and won't invest the latter, you're in trouble.

Jacques an' Claude Thibodaux, dey was two brothers who lived in New Orleans. Dey worked at Etienne's, a little restaurant out by Tulane. Jacques, he was a cook an' Claude, he was a waiter. Dose two boys, dey doan like cookin' an' waitin' very much, and dey was expectin' life to make them millinionaires.

Dey thought life done come through when news come dat dere Grandpere Clesma had died and left 'em a 40 acres farm near Rayne, up in Cajun country. Clesma, he was a good farmer, but he didn't spend a lot of money. He never bought any tractors and used mules and a middle buster plow 'til the day he died. If you doan know what is a middle buster plow, watch de TV show "Little Prairie on de House."

Anyway, Clesma's plowin' mule had died. So, Jacques and Claude went to town to get another one. Now, Jacques had some cash money from his restaurant job, an' not many people in dem days did. Also, de boys knew 'bout cookin' an' waitin', an' dey done figgered out dat dey doan like many tings 'bout farmin'. Dey get to de mule barn and Jacques say, "Claude, you wait here on de wagon an' I'll go get us a deal on a plowin' mule." Jacques, he went into de barn an' doggone, de mule barn people, dey ain't got no full-grown plowin' mules!

Man, de clerk run to de back, said, "Boss, Jacques and Claude Thibodaux here and Jacques, he out dere wid a handful of New Orleans cash money; we ain't got no plowin' mule!" Boss say, "Well, doan you worry 'bout dat, Ah'll take care of de Thibodaux boys."

De boss tell de clerk, "You see dose two watermelons in de corner, take dem an' whitewash 'em." Den de boss he walk in de front, put his arm around Jacques an' say,

"Come on, Jacques, we gonna drink some coffee." He say, "Jacques, Ah got a deal for you, it's so good, you ain't gonna believe it!

"Tell you what Ah'm gonna do....for de same cash money, me, instead of sellin' you one mule, Ah'm gonna sell you two mule eggs!"

Jacques said, "Two mule eggs?"

Boss say, "Yea, Jacques, an' dey is about ready to hatch! Dese is real special mule eggs. Can you tink, Jacques, how many mules you two is goin' to own when dese mules lay eggs? You and Claude will be de mule kings of south Louisiana!"

Jacques said, "Hole youself, I got to ask Claude 'bout dat."

Jacques, he go back out to de wagon an' say, "Claude, de boss, he wants to sell us two mule eggs instead of one full grown plowin' mule. He say when dese mules hatch and lay eggs, we is gonna' be de mule kings of south Louisiana! "

"...de mule eggs roll out on de dirt road."

Claude said, "Jump on dat, boy, dat's a good deal!" Well, dey got dere mule eggs an' put dem in de back of de wagon, but dey forgot to close de tailgate on de wagon. In a little while, dey come on a little rise in de road and de mule eggs roll out on de dirt road

Jacques jumped out de wagon and run after his mule eggs, but dey roll faster than he could run an' went into de woods, hit a tree an' busted into little pieces. Now, in de woods dere was two little rabbits and dey come out an' start eatin' dose watermelons. Jacques saw dat an' hollered to Claude, "Come help me boy, our mule eggs done hatched an' we got two baby mules. You oughta see de ears on dem tings!"

Man, dey start runnin' after dem rabbits, through de briar brushes, over de fence, trough de canal; of course, they never caught 'em. Jacques was clean bushed and sat down on a stump and wiped de sweat off his face and tried to catch his breath. Claude looked down at him and said, "Hot dog, Ah hate dat not only you lost you cash money, now you done lost you baby mules, too."

Jacques look back at him and said, "Well, Claude, doan feel too bad about dat, cause to tell you de truth, Ah didn't want to plow dat fast anyhow."

"You oughta see de ears on dem tings!"

AMBUSH AT HONEYSUCKLE STOOP

MERWYN BRIAN PETTYJOHN

Most sentient beings require only a tap on the shoulder from God. Others need reminding in a more pointed, forceful manner.

Sandstone, Texas, was, on the surface, a plain town, even drab. Lurking under that drab patina, however, were people with the same hopes, dreams, and fears we all have. Life went on there with a patient, stolid expectation, assuming you live by the Golden Rule and work hard, that the coming years would bring approximately the same measure of happiness and prosperity that was always experienced there. It was in that environment that Mildred B. Clements started her second marriage. Her first hadn't been a happy one and with a quiet, plain-spoken determination, she assumed the matriarchal duties of her new home.

She was an inveterate cultivator of roses, taking pride in not only their appearance as lovely blooms, but in her rose garden's role as an adjunct floral decoration of her new home. She regarded the roses with a maternal ferocity bordering on obsession.

All the neighborhood children knew that the creation of the slightest danger or inconvenience for her roses, however innocently done, was simply unacceptable behavior and involved the possibility of punishment that could be unimaginably severe.

There was a large bed of roses just outside her back door. It was in that precise location for purposes of the garden's security as much as it was from a horticultural point of view. Overlooking the garden was a small, covered stoop located just outside her back door. The stoop had wooden lattice-work trellises painted white on which were growing in wild profusion her second most favorite flower, red honeysuckle. They thrived under her constant care and feeding and soon enclosed the porch with a wall of lush green leaves and beautiful, pale red honeysuckle blossoms with golden stamens.

She trimmed a doorway in this honeysuckle wall for access to her rose garden, located about fifteen feet down a sandstone sidewalk from the stoop. She positioned her favorite lawn chair inside her cool, green-walled observation point and, on hot summer days, would sit in that chair, outfitted in her softly patterned cotton day dress, sipping hot mint tea, drifting in and out of short, dreamy naps, smelling the aroma of the honeysuckle blooms and looking out at her beloved roses.

A pall fell over Sandstone's horticultural Eden one summer in the person's of new neighbors, Pearl and Orville Wilson and their short-haired, male bird dog, Sam.

Mildred had two serious problems with the Wilsons. First, she discovered that neither Pearl nor Orville had any love for flowers when they "planted" 30 plastic geraniums with blue blossoms across the front flower bed of their home. From Mildred's point of view, that affront was roughly akin to attending church naked. Second, and much more serious, was Sam's behavior.

In the absence of a system of fireplugs in Sandstone, Sam adopted Mildred's rose garden as the locale for canine relief. Mildred mumbled about decreasing real estate values and the collapse of society in general. She also said she was losing weight chasing Sam from the rose garden. They were both implacable in their resolve.

It was about a month after the Wilsons moved in that Mildred's husband, Richard, discovered an air powered pellet pistol hidden in her knitting bag. He asked her what she planned to use the gun for and she simply stared at him, hesitated a moment, and said "Rats." She glared at Richard, daring him to challenge her answer. Field mice were common around Sandstone, but he had never seen any rats and told her so. She nodded her head in agreement, stared at him a moment more before dropping her gaze and looked out the window. He had lived with her long enough to know that their conversation had just ended. She didn't want to talk about the pellet gun.

The following Saturday after the discovery of the gun, Richard had some friends over to watch football on television. Mildred was not a fan of college football; she preferred the blue and silver of the Dallas Cowboys, and so was on her stoop enjoying the solitude and quiet of the afternoon.

A commercial break had just flashed on the television screen so Richard muted the sound and they sat back to wait. Suddenly they heard a dog howling just outside the back window. The noises they heard indicated the dog was experiencing severe discomfort. They ran to the window just in time to see Sam, the Wilson's bird dog, dashing out the far end of Mildred's rose garden. Sam would run a few feet, stop, run in circles, bite at his own rear end, and then run a few more feet before repeating his whirling dervish imitation.

"The pellet pistol was still in her hand."

Realizing that Mildred was on the back stoop, the men ran to the back door to see if she was all right. She was sitting in her chair which had been positioned next to a hole she had made in the honeysuckle vine. She could see her rose bushes through the hole without being observed by trespassers. The pellet pistol was still in her hand. She looked up at the men as they poured out the back door onto the stoop. Her eyes challenged each of the men to object to what she had obviously just done. The men just stood and stared, some with nearly invisible smiles on their faces. With no approval forthcoming, she arose from her chair and, holding the muzzle of the pistol up, she blew away some imaginary smoke and , with the air of a grim-faced hit woman, jammed the pistol back into her knitting bag. She passed brusquely by the men on her way into the house with the comment, "That sunuvabitch won't be peeing on anything for a day or two!"

"She never fired the gun again."

THE FLIGHT OF THE CONDOR

MERWYN BRIAN PETTYJOHN

To fly...to escape the surly bonds of Earth is, at some time in his life, the dream of most boys. Some even do, but also discover that overreaching ambition is fraught with peril.

Nineteen forty-four was a memorable year. Trey was nine years old and his brother John six when their father took them to Fort Worth to see the technological marvel of the age, a fighter plane. They had seen glimpses of them overhead; they were the ones whose sound lagged behind in the sky. Both of them were fascinated with combat aircraft, a love encouraged when their uncle, for some reason unbeknownst to them, purchased two gutted WWII, single engine training aircraft and parked them at his Indian Creek farm. They "flew" hundreds of combat missions in those old wrecks and were both aces before the summer was over.

Indian Creek was on the southern edge of the Eagle Mountain Navy Base which during the war was the site of seaplane pilot training. On family excursions to Indian Creek, they had watched the big, ungainly PBY aircraft take off and land on the lake. The thunder of those engines caressed their ears as the seaplanes raced along the surface of the lake, straining toward the sky. Trey and John often rode their uncle's horse through the woods to the hangars and watched those squat, fat seaplanes waddle out of the hangar and down the ramp into the lake. They were there at the edge of the tarmac one day when one of the crew, probably a maintenance technician, called to them and motioned them over to a PBY whose engines were running but didn't seem to be going anywhere. They walked their horse across the tarmac, two very different worlds meeting in a most improbable scene.

"Trey and John often rode their uncle's horse through the woods to the hangars..."

He said, "I've seen you boys watching this hangar and our planes several days now." They nodded their assent of his observation. He looked at them with a hard stare, "You're not spies, are you?" He put a melodramatic emphasis on "spies." "Oh, no, sir," was their chorused reply. Trey said, "We just like to watch the planes take off and land." The airman nodded his head understandingly, hesitated a moment, freezing the boys in place with a serious stare, and said, "Would you like to see the inside of one?" They gaped at him in disbelief that such a thing could be possible. Their faces could hardly accommodate larger smiles as they immediately agreed. "Well, pile down off that cayuse and come on with me; I have to do some taxi testing with that one right there." They hitched their horse to the hangar's flagpole and followed him to the plane.

They had no idea what "taxi testing" was and so were astounded when, after hearing the engine run-up, the plane actually began to move! The noise was deafening and the excitement was nearly unbearable. They were in a warplane and they were moving! The plane never got off the ground; it went to the end of the runway and back to the hangar. Their friends at school would never believe this! They thanked their host profusely, retrieved their horse and started back to Indian Creek. They reached the edge of the tarmac and, reluctant to return to their normal, everyday world, turned for one more look at "their" PBY.

The half mile ride in a pot-bellied PBY had totally hooked them on aviation. It occupied every conversation for days after that ride. Back home at Windwhistle Ranch, they slipped into their normal routine, but the memory of their "flight" lurked near the surface of every thought. For years they painted glamorous accounts of the ride to all their friends. One of their school chums, Ronnie Turnage, was mesmerized by their description of the aircraft noises, the smell of the fuel, but especially of their account of soaring over Eagle Mountain Lake and what everything looked like from the air. It was with this fascination in mind that they formed a partnership with Ronnie to create their own airship.

Ronnie was short, but in the manner of many Texas-born, hard as a rock. He was elected, because of his size, to be the pilot. He was thrilled. The boys set about considering their airship's design and immediately encountered the same problems that all serious aircraft designers worry over: pilot safety, structural integrity of the aircraft, speed, lift, and propulsion. They had failed to consider another problem, the cost of building such an airship. The solution to one problem led to the solution of another, and the determination of the designers took them far beyond the bounds of good sense. They named their aircraft "The Condor" because of the wide wingspread they had determined necessary to actually fly. They had never actually seen a condor, but had found a picture of one in the library.

They realized, early on in the design phase, that they were limited in many ways. They had no practical method of propulsion. Their solution was to make The Condor a glider. They were worried about pilot safety so Ronnie brought his older brother Larry's football shoulder pads and helmet. They were certain that these devices would protect Ronnie should some unexpected disaster befall The Condor. The next problem they solved was the weight and structural integrity of the aircraft. Nearly all the farms and ranches nearby had some old, broken down aluminum lawn furniture. They put the word out and within a few days had a veritable boneyard of discarded aluminum skeletons at the rear of the barn.

Project Condor was begun! They realized that lift was a serious problem, since there was no propulsion. They read the high school physics book chapter on air foils and felt that they had the lift problem solved. They had pictures of single-wing Cessna and Piper aircraft, gleaned from library periodicals.

The sight of three deadly serious small boys hunched over aviation magazines and copying sketches must have been a source of amusement for the librarian. No matter to serious engineers. They noted that the Cessnas had supports built from the fuselage to the wings ("fuselage" was a new word which they adopted to demonstrate their level of technical expertise to Whitt's uninitiated). Not to be outdone by Cessna, they incorporated the wing support idea into The Condor. That decision made possible the singular triumph of their experience; the wings didn't fall off.

The pictures they used as design blueprints showed the outside of the aircraft skin but, not being intended as builders' specifications, omitted some important details about airframe construction. The lack of propulsive power turned out to be a blessing in disguise. They used their father's drill, a lot of nuts and bolts, and several lengths of 1" x 2" lumber to create the skeleton of The Condor. They left intact one of the better chaise lounges with plastic netting and, with a bottle of Coca-Cola, christened it as the First Officer's seat. They used half the bottle for that purpose and then, as an afterthought, each took a small drink as a toast and used the rest to christen The Condor. It was a deadly serious ceremony. Why the title of First Officer was chosen is lost to history, for there was no room for a Second Officer.

The next problem was the wings. The boys approached Mrs. Taylor at the Whitt Store with the problem, telling her they were making a "kite." She suggested one of the new synthetics. They ordered twenty yards. "Twenty yards!" she exclaimed, "How big of a kite are you making?"

"Pretty big" was their answer, and they put all the money they had amassed on the counter.

"You boys are about $3.00 short," she said. Seeing the crestfallen looks on their faces, she added, "You can come in and pay me later, I believe I can trust you three." They arrived back at Windwhistle with the bolt of material and began work.

Trey and John told their mother that we were making a big kite and needed help sewing the wings. Though they didn't realize it at the time, that was another of those fortuitous decisions which saved Ronnie from possible injury. She reinforced the seams using fishing line which would not fail under stress. The wingspread of The Condor was impressive, sixteen feet across and four feet wide. They had inadvertently told Mrs. Taylor the truth. They had built a kite. They tried to curve the wing to create an airfoil but hadn't reckoned with the material's flapping instead of remaining rigid. They nailed a long strip of corrugated tin on the barn roof to use as a runway. Their collective experience with flying had to do with paper airplanes.

Even a beginning paper airplane maker knows the value of weight in the nose. It provides a nose-down attitude allowing the plane to gather enough speed to swoop and soar. They incorporated that concept into The Condor. Ronnie would be stationed just forward of amidships in his chaise lounge. Because they underestimated the "success" of the coming flight, they made the erroneous assumption that flaps and other control surfaces would not be necessary.

"Flight testing" was accomplished by attaching a rope from Trey's saddlehorn to the nose of the plane and pulling it pilotless across the pasture with John and Ronnie holding it up by the wing struts. When they ran into the wind, it actually lifted out of their hands. It only occurred to them later that Trey's pulling the plane provided not only propulsion, but direction. Ronnie's older brother gave him one of his old t-shirts to wear on the flight.

The day finally came for manned flight testing. The prevailing winds at Windwhistle were westerly so they had positioned the tin strip on the barn roof to take advantage of them. The Condor had the wheels from John's Radio Flyer wagon as landing gear. They were just narrower, wheel-to-wheel, than the tin strip down which The Condor would be rolling on takeoff. Ronnie was becoming nervous as flight time approached and observed that he had no way to guide the plane down the strip. Trey and John assured him, not convincingly, that because of the corrugations in the tin, The Condor would simply roll straight down the barn roof "runway," become airborne, and all he had to do was shift his weight from side to side, or front to back, depending on which way he wanted to go. Ronnie shook his head, understanding what they said, but lacking the confidence of a true believer. John and Trey glanced at each other, suspecting that their First Officer was teetering on the edge of mutiny.

They hurried to ready The Condor, tying a rope to Trey's horse's saddle horn and stationed him in the middle of the corral, on the other side of the barn away from The Condor's scheduled flight path, next to the pile of cow manure. John threw the end of the rope over the barn and tied it to the Condor's tail. With John and Ronnie helping on the takeoff side of the barn, Trey walked his horse slowly away from the barn, hoisting The Condor, tail-first, onto the roof and up the tin strip to the roof's peak. The Condor had a "brake" in the form of a movable metal strip protruding down from the plane, catching the peak of the barn. John and Ronnie engaged the brake and The Condor was poised to fly!

At its vantage point on the barn's roof, The Condor was visible from Windwhistle's ranch house. It was time for lunch and their mother called them in, noting The Condor on the barn's roof. She asked, "What is that thing doing on the barn?" They told her they were going to fly it that afternoon. She said, "Just be sure it's off the barn when your father comes home."

By the time they were outside again, the wind had come up sharply and The Condor was creaking and groaning from the top of the barn. The Condor's signs of nervousness were matched by those of its First Officer. In an effort to breathe confidence into Ronnie, Trey said, "Ronnie, you need a title, and I have just the one!. Do you remember the story our teacher read us about Jason?" He nodded nervously that he did, never taking his eyes off the quivering Condor. Trey said, "I think your title ought to be 'Aeronaut'!" That diverted Ronnie's attention from The Condor long enough for Trey to press his point home. "I can just see the headline now....'Ronnie Turnage, Aeronaut, tests new type glider!'"

Ronnie looked from John to Trey, momentarily awash in possible glory, when a sudden gust of wind caused The Condor to creak menacingly atop the barn.

The spell broken, Ronnie said, "Yeah, I can see the headline, too... Ronnie Turnage, dumb ass Aeronaut, killed falling off barn in an experimental aircraft made of scrap lumber and lawn furniture!" They calmed Ronnie by suggesting that they letter "AERONAUT" on his t-shirt. This gesture, helped by the fact that the wind was dying down, coming in gusts instead of a steady blow, had a calming effect on the Aeronaut.

Up the ladder Ronnie and John went. John was to Release the brake on Ronnie's command, and Trey was on the ground in the barnyard, directing John to move the tail of The Condor to assure a straight roll down the tin strip.

Ronnie looked grim in the oversized Aeronaut t-shirt, ballooned by his brother's shoulder pads. His brother's football helmet was several sizes too large, too, and kept sliding over his eyes. Reclining on the First Officer's chaise lounge, the enormity of what he was about to do hit him. He was staring straight ahead with round eyes and quivering lips. He looked down in the barnyard at the now-small figure of Trey who shouted encouragement. A sickly smile spread across Ronnie's face. Events were spiraling out of his control. There was a struggle going on in his mind. He judged that his choice was suicide or cowardice. He chose the former.

John adjusted the direction of The Condor to Trey's satisfaction, and Trey gave Ronnie the "Go" sign.

Ronnie hesitated, took a deep breath, exhaled and cried, "Brake off!" The Condor began her roll. Halfway down the roof of the barn, The Condor lurched to the right and Ronnie shifted quickly to the left.

"...lifting The Condor and the screaming Aeronaut

His oversized football helmet fell over his eyes. He screamed that he was blind, but he had no way of stopping The Condor.

Just as the plane's nose reached the edge of the barn, an incredibly strong gust of wind arrived, lifting The Condor and the screaming Aeronaut straight up but in level flight.

...straight up but in level flight."

The Condor and the wind were in a battle. The boys had designed The Condor to be slightly nose-heavy and, true to its builders, the aircraft's nose kept dipping. As soon as it did, the wind would get under the wing and lift it higher. With no method of forward propulsion, these two forces produced a relatively level, but porpoising flight with The Condor facing the proper direction but, in fact, flying backwards.

Ronnie was holding on with one hand and trying to right his football helmet with the other. His screams degenerated from intelligible words to a long, uninterrupted scream, "Oh! Oh, my! Oh, God! Oh, God! Oh, No! Oh, Noooo, YAAAAAGGHHHHH!" As The Condor rose over the barn's roof, it narrowly missed John, who ducked, lost his footing and slid down the tin strip, catching himself just before he would have fallen off.

Trey was shocked. He couldn't move. As The Condor rose above the peak in the barn's roof, it lost some of the fierce lift the wind gust was providing and did precisely what it was designed to do, dropped its nose and dove. It disappeared from Trey's view and the sounds of Ronnie's screams and twisted metal came from over the barn.

The Condor had been lifted by the gust of wind, flown backwards over the barn and lost its lift. It dove nose-first into the pile of cow manure, crushing the entire front of the fragile craft and ejecting the Aeronaut face first. While John was climbing down the ladder, Trey raced around the barn to discover the Aeronaut's fate and that of The Condor. The Aeronaut had fared much the better of the two.

"...the sputtering, spitting Ronnie was covered in cow manure."

Ronnie's football helmet and chaise lounge chair had protected him from injury, but not from the cow manure. He had pitched directly forward into it upon impact and had from any further contact with The Condor. Trey and John rushed up, exclaiming to Ronnie what a magnificent flight he had made and that they would correct the design flaws for the next one. In that the sputtering, spitting Ronnie was covered in cow manure, it was difficult to do with straight faces.

He looked at Trey and John as if not quite believing what they were suggesting and said curtly, “Screw you.”

It was The Condor’s last flight. The boys lived without aviation for a number of years.

"His left hand graspin' hard the rein, his right one soft the rose."

THE TAMIN' OF LILLIAN SUE

MERWYN BRIAN PETTYJOHN

She was only a girl from the social swirl,
Her name was Lillian Sue.
With a figure prime and a face sublime,
And a life with nuthin' to do.

Her azure eyes and hair of gold,
Covered up a soul so bare,
She'd a fickle streak that made men weak,
But Lillian didn't care.

Her mother's name was Patty,
Her daddy's name was Bill.
Her lover's name was David James,
Of him she'd had her fill.

The kind of man who scared her,
A mix of soft and strong.
A feathery touch which said so much,
She knew she wasn't wrong.

One night he came a-callin',
The ride was nigh ten miles.
His horse was wet with salty sweat,
His face was wreathed in smiles.

His soul was nearly poppin',
As he galloped o'er the hill.
His heart could melt with the love he felt,
When he thought about his Lil.

The rose he held so tenderly,
His fingers round it closed.
His left hand graspin' hard the rein,
His right one soft the rose.

He stepped upon the front yard stoop,
And stalled around until,
He slicked his hair and said a prayer,
And thought upon his Lil.

He was askin' for her hand tonight,
Couldn't figure how to start.
He counted five and then to ten,
Tryin' to calm his throbbin' heart.

He tapped the door so timidly,
That Bill could barely hear.
The beads of sweat in rivulets met.
His eyes were wide with fear.

Bill cracked the door and looked outside,
And when their gazes met,
He grabbed Dave's hand with gesture grand,
And told him come and set.

Now, Pat and Bill, they liked this boy,
Who's callin' on their Lil.
This honest flame named David James,
Of him she'd had her fill.

They sat him on the sofa,
With hands between his knees.
He had to say why he came that day,
Strivin' mightily to please.

Bill and Patty waited there,
To hear what he would say.
This honest flame named David James,
Who called on Lil that day.

He started, "Bill and Patty,
Here's what I aim to do.
I'm a decent sort and with all my heart,
I'll marry Lillian Sue."

Bill and Patty stared a bit,
And shared a furtive glance.
They turned and squirmed and wiggle-wormed,
About this boy's romance.

"Lillian's upstairs in her room,"
Her dad began to say.
And with a frown, "she's not been down,
Forever and a day!"

"She'll set up there in her underwear,
And scream and yell and cuss.
And if you aim to marry her,
You'll be worse off than us!"

But David's love for Lillian Sue,
Had no mete nor line.
He plucked his will and said to Bill,
"Good sir, I'll make her mine!"

He started up the stairway,
The blood-red rose in hand.
He turned to look and the petals shook,
But he stuck flat to his plan.

He strode right to her doorway,
And nearly knocked it down.
He slammed the boards and fairly roared.
There stood Lillian in her gown.

"With a round-house right she missed."

A one-eyed squint she gave to him,
With a round-house right she missed.
She whirled around in her flannel gown,
With a drunken sailor's list

Dave grabbed her on the second turn,
And said, "you'll be mine, Lil."
She kicked his shin and bit his chin,
And said, "the hell I will!"

Now David James was a gentle man,
Good manners, that an' all.
But an achin' shin and a bleedin' chin,
Wuz way beyond the call.

So he twirled her one more time around,
Flung her face-down on the bed.
One hand held her behind down,
The other held her head.

She yelled and screamed and spit and snarled,
And told how he would die.
He gave a frown and held her down,
And said, "Now there you'll lie!"

Now David James was an honest man,
Tried and faithful and true.
So when he said, "You'll stay in bed,"
That's exactly what she'd do!

Lillian didn't like that much,
And forcefully told him so.
With a plaintive cry and eructal sigh,
Her dignity let go.

That overturned his ticklebox,
And ended their little spat.
He laughed too hard, let down his guard,
And on the floor he sat.

She punched him in the stomach,
And kicked him 'tween the hips.
She pinched his ears and brought on tears,
Then kissed him on the lips.

"David James, I am your Lil,
But if you throw me down again,
I'll slap your face and change your bass,
And bite you on the chin!"

Now David James was a gentle man,
Good manners, that and all.
So he brushed her hair and cheek so fair,
And stepped out in the hall.

He looked back through the doorway,
And said, "I love you sweet."
"But if you ever bite my chin again,
I'll knock you off your feet."

They married soon thereafter,
As we always knew they'd do.
True enough, the goin' was rough,
For the tamin' of Lillian Sue.

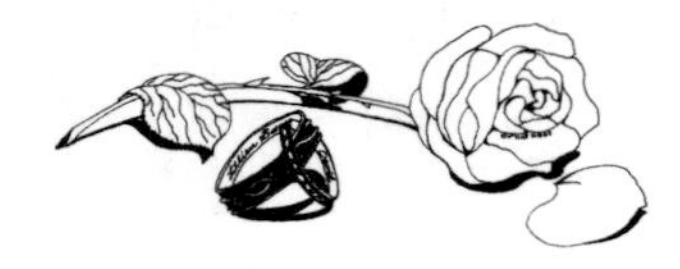

"True enough, the goin' was rough, For the tamin' of Lillian Sue."

BELL, POL AND MISS BIRD

LYNN VEACH SADLER

The neighbors surmised that Abner Murray had bought the parrot for his niece. His law practice was on the coast, and they reasoned that some sailor had returned from a voyage with it to sell. Why Abner thought its vocabulary was suited to his old-maid niece, Miss Essie, could not be surmised.

Ever perverse, Miss Essie had taken to the bird, and "Pol" became a fixture of her household. On warm days, he was to be seen in his cage, on a pedestal stand on the back porch. At night, she carried his covered cage up to her bedroom. She liked to hear the clucking noises he made deep down in his throat. She taught Pol the proper parts of "Polly Wolly Doodle All Day," replete with a fair mimicry of her own breathless lift between words.

Pol heightened the neighborhood's awareness of Miss Essie as a "character." For many years, whenever she'd need help, she rang the huge dinner bell hanging over the back porch (though no one could remember it ever being used to summon people to eat). It would bong for a good ten minutes, and, in accordance with country etiquette, the neighbors up to three miles away would answer the distress signal. From their point of view, the summonses were for trivial matters—when Miss Essie's companion, Rowena Smith, didn't get home from a foraging expedition early enough to suit her; when a cow broke out of the pasture; when her ancient Essex had a flat tire; when somebody "stole" her milk pail; when she couldn't get the pump primed...Now these little episodes were more dramatic—Pol squawked and called for help as soon as Miss Essie or Rowena rang the bell. He truly was quite piercing and Miss Essie learned to insert cotton in her ears before she gave him the signal to cut loose.

The side porch that connected the main part of Miss Essie's house with the kitchen area faced toward the Litchfield Patterson place, so the Pattersons received the greatest benefit from Miss Essie's dinner bell and parrot. After a bell-ringing, Mrs. Patterson would declare, "I don't know what that woman is thinking of. She must not ever had heard of Peter and the Wolf."

The Patterson child, nicknamed "Miss Bird," was determined to get a close-up look at a real bird. Entranced with the idea of this creature, she infuriated her no-nonsense father by chanting, ever faster, in mimicry of Miss Essie's style, "Bell-ring, Pol-call, peo-ple come; bell-ring, pol-call, peo-ple come!"

The community did once get a little of its own back. Miss Essie had, as always, exacted a kiss on the mouth as the bribe for letting Pol out of his cage that morning. Ancient and crotchety, he had perhaps decided that enough was enough.

He bit his mistress on the nose and wouldn't let go. Rowena couldn't break his grip, so she had to turn to the bell to summon help, and everyone had scrambled to the rescue.

"Now, Miss Essie," Litchfield Patterson told her, in great solemnity of tone and with much commiseration, "I've heard tell—you probably have, too—a parrot won't let go until it thunders.

Miss Bird was instantly into correction: "No, Daddy, it's a terrapin, not a parrot, that won't let go until—" Her mother grabbed her by the arm, stepped on her foot and shushed her.

"...Rowena couldn't break his grip, so she had to turn to the bell to summon help..."

At any rate, when the bell stopped, Pol was soothed down enough to release his hold on the proboscis.

When Mrs. Patterson did her accustomed duty and deposited Miss Essie at Dr. Mack's office in town, the woman grudgingly admitted: "My-par-rot-bite-me!"

For months all the local wags greeted Dr. Mack with, "Hey, Doc, cured any parrot bites lately?"

Back home afterwards, Mr. Patterson stated unequivocally: "Old Pol's beak rivals his owner's. That's probably what the ruckus was about in the first place!"

He and his wife laughed and laughed, though she was cautionary: "Now, Litchfield! You shouldn't say such things in front of our little pitcher."

Miss Bird laughed, too, but she secretly vowed to measure the two noses in question. She was a stickler for facts.

IF I'M ANY JUDGE

LYNN VEACH SADLER

I knew mama would say, "Now Jean-Anne, didn't I tell you so?" but didn't expect her to start up the instant things went wrong.

I was seventeen. I'd wanted to be an "aviator pilot" since I had been knee-high to a kitten, as Daddy put it.

It was Daddy who finally said, "Now, Maudie Lou," which is what he called mama, "leave the child be. We've got us one child out of nine that ain't clear of nature, but is mixed, if I'm any judge. Jean-Anne will do what she pleases all of her life, if I'm any judge. I do not claim to know God's intentions when it came to making Jean-Anne, but she'll be free to live in accord with what the Good Lord intended for her. If she can come to find out what that is. And she will, if I'm any judge."

Daddy's favorite expression was "if I'm any judge." I've liked it since the first time I noticed him saying it. I've used "if I'm any judge" on my own occasions.

Daddy put his foot down on mama and bought me a parachuting ride for graduating a year early. He drove me to Seymour Air Force Base one afternoon where a friend of his in "Operations" had arranged for me to be taken up. Just Daddy and I went. There wasn't room in the car for the whole family, and Daddy didn't want to be choosy. I'd rigged this special costume for the occasion. All white. A blouse, pedal pushers, white socks and tennis shoes. I wanted a big billowy skirt and puffed sleeves, but settled for mama's white silk shawl I sneaked out of the house under my blouse. Mama insisted I pigtail my hair so it wouldn't get in my eyes and blind me, and I did it without fussing, knowing just what I'd do when the time came.

Despite Daddy's friend Mr. Pridgen fussing over me and saying I could back out and no harm done, the time did come. I was disappointed in a way because the plane was not a spiffy fighter type, more like a crop duster you might fly over White Lake in for $10.00 to get an aerial perspective. The pilot was called "The Moose" and chewed tobacco. He was going to keep at it right through the flight, if I was any judge. I could picture him cutting loose as I went out of the plane and mucking up my white outfit. The Moose stood by chewing and spitting and looking me up and down. He was making a game of how close he could come, if I'm any judge. But Daddy saw I was getting nervous and made The Moose move off a bit. Mr. Pridgen and another man "checked me out on the art of parachuting," but I knew more than they showed they knew because I had read all about it in the County Library. I had to tell them the "how-do-you-call-it" was a rip cord. Finally, they gave up on me, after practicing in and out of the plane, on the ground, of course, because Mr. Pridgen's friend said I had more smarts than a regular male pilot.

The Moose just kept staring at me and spitting his tobacco juice. I knew he was going to make mischief. Which he did. He showed himself as soon as we were off the ground, doing loops and making figure eights and causing the engine to misfire at which he yelled the f-word at me using the word itself. I loved it, but The Moose reached the point where he was looking what daddy called "green around the gills." Finally, he screamed, "To hell with you Girlie!" (and was not the last man to do so, be assured). Get out of my plane!"

I was standing in position for my jump when he yelled that, and he yawed and jerked, and I just tumbled out. Right then was when mama kicked in with her, "Now Jean-Anne, didn't I tell you so?" Which made me even madder at The Moose and put the stiffening right back into my backbone, for I do admit to being uncomfortable at the turn of events. At first. Then I saw The Moose looking out and laughing at me and spitting in my direction, and I just arced myself up and gave him the finger and went right on with my original intentions. I pulled the cord and the jerk was followed by the most perfect peace I have almost ever known. While that beautiful white canopy was arranging itself, like a living blessing right over my head, I pulled the rubber bands out of my pigtails and let my hair go free. Then I reached under my blouse for mama's shawl and let it flow out behind me. And it was all Kingdom Come and the Sweet Now and Now. Only—-

Only it was over too soon and plonked me in my own special Brier Patch. I couldn't blame The Moose because he didn't have the gumption to land me where I landed. Which was this giant pecan tree. I was not a stranger to such. Daddy had made us a swing attached to one, and all of us nine children had pulled picking-up-pecans duty. But pecan limbs don't grow low on the tree in the first place, and this was humongous. I thought I was going to squeeze by without upsetting that tree, but my shawl snagged it, and mama started up again with her "Now Jean-Anne." I was so irked to hear it, I lost concentration. Then there I was, "Wham, bam, thank you, Mr. Pecan Tree."

When I stopped struggling and took stock, I knew I'd crack too many parts if I tried dropping to the ground. The parachute was snug in the tree, so I flipped myself down enough, in my rigging, to peek at the trunk. It must have been the closest we had to a California Redwood. I couldn't begin to straddle it and descend like a telephone lineman, assuming I managed to get where bare trunk began. I tried yelling, but no one came. When I got hoarse, I stopped and made something of a nest of the parachute. I tied mama's shawl to a strap of it and carefully pushed it outside the leaves as a signal. I wished I had a black crayon to draw an SOS on it. I guess my battles with The Moose had taken their toll because I went to sleep, rousing up and dozing off again the whole night through.

At daylight, I woke abruptly to a whole lot of tree shaking going on. I could hear green pecans falling and thudding softly on the ground. I wanted to focus on the image of the raining pecan pods, but was too curious about what caused the shaking.

You won't believe this, but it was a young man in a pilot's uniform and a red parachute by which he was held up in the branches. He was still swinging back and forth and had to use his feet to rappel himself away or get mushed into the trunk.

He looked up at me whenever he could afford to look away. "I've come to rescue you!" he called up. "Lt. Whitman

Ford Whittle at your service, Miss. Call me 'Whit.' You've stirred up a hornet's nest. From what The Moose said about you, I figured you were worth finding. My co-pilot and I saw your signal. Pretty smart." He meant mama's shawl.

"I've come to rescue you!"

"How're you going to save me?" I yelled down at him.

"Just watch me!"

With that, he swung up to sit on the limb above him, unhooked and dropped his parachute, which was wearing its heart on its sleeve, if I'm any judge, and came climbing up after me. If I'm any judge. He set off a smoke signal and I ate the candy bars he'd brought along while we waited for his plane to send somebody for us.

We married eight months later after Whit taught me to fly and I had my license. He stayed in the Air Force, but we opened a crop-dusting service and flight school on land Daddy gave us. I ran the business while Whit was away. Mama took to him immediately. He made a big thing in the papers about her being smart enough to send along her shawl in case I needed a "beacon." My whole family was in the news. Mama loved it. Daddy, too, if I'm any judge.

After Whit was shot down in Vietnam, I worked on teaching every mother's daughter I could get my hands on to fly. One of these days, when I go down, Whit will come, dressed in his red parachute, to fly us both to the Sweet By and By, if God is any judge.

ONE TALE, TWO TAILS...

LYNN VEACH SADLER

People said Aunt Juliana never met a man she didn't hate, a cat she didn't love. The only thing she resented about being an old-maid school teacher was the stereotype.

Aunt Juliana and Mayor Bob Hargrove had been sweethearts. Not even mother, her sister, knew what parted them. Aunt Juliana never spoke to (or voted for) him after that. He married the next prettiest girl in their class, but after mother told me about their "blighted love," I watched Mr. Bob watch Aunt Juliana. She never cut him an ion of slack, left the room when my parents mentioned him. When his wife died, we bet on how long it would be before he came sniffing around. He invited himself to Sunday dinner, which Aunt Juliana took with us, three months to the day after Mrs. Hargrove was buried.

When Aunt Juliana saw him, she excused herself, calling over her shoulder as she high-nosed out, "The day Jubal talks is the day I sit down with Robert Hargrove!" That was Aunt Juliana's version of "when hell freezes over."

We sat around the table discussing how Mr. Bob could ingratiate himself with Aunt Juliana. Over the bread pudding with whiskey sauce we always had on Sundays, my brother and me included, father said, "Well, Bob, there's only one way to win Juliana. Make Jubal talk." We laughed, but I watched Mr. Bob tuck the idea away.

Jubal was Aunt Juliana's most beloved cat. She had saved him when her neighbors were going to drown him. He was retarded, the runt in a litter of five Persians. One eye was green; one yellow ringed with black and then blue. He was more cross-eyed than a Siamese. Wall-eyed, father said, out of Aunt Juliana's hearing. Worse, Jubal had two tails, both beautiful-regular-big Persian, but if he didn't keep them straight up, he'd tip to one side, and when they were straight up, his front end rode high, and he'd be clawing air. Jubal didn't move around much, probably for that very tail problem.

The worst, for Aunt Juliana, was that Jubal never meowed, not even as a day-old kitten. What a sad state of affairs when a kitten/cat didn't make his God-given sounds. She took him to Doc Martin, the vet, who deemed Jubal's problem "psychological." Aunt Juliana tried three psychiatrists. They'd treat her, not her cat; she left miffed. The wags claimed that she had finally decided to let sleeping cats lie.

But I had seen Mr. Bob's whatever-it-takes look. He became a regular at our house, "aiming to prepare for a smooth transition into the family if the opportunity arose." My parents thought Aunt Juliana deserved connubial bliss and aided-abetted. Mr. Bob powwowed with Doc, then bought Popeye Turner's best coon dog, naming him "Riches" and promising we'd know why if things worked out. Doc, Mr. Bob and Popeye trained him.

The Big Day was February 14, Valentines having been when Mr. Bob and Juliana parted. It was also the annual date she opened her home to animals, spending weeks preparing heart- and Cupid-shaped treats, not just for cats, dogs, parakeets, parrots, foxes, squirrels, turtles and goldfish, but for whatever your pet was. She had entertained iguanas, monkeys, lion cubs..... The state zoo sent exotic specimens to her "Animal Fete." There was a lot of publicity, including TV. If only Mr. Bob could have notified Oprah about this one.....

Everybody but my Aunt knew about Mr. Bob's "secret," but not its nature. Aunt Juliana had the family place, which was, blessedly, big. The town was there early, but Mr. Bob arrived precisely half-way through, with Doc behind him. Everyone went quiet when they appeared in the doorway. Animals, too; Aunt Juliana always praised them for their sixth sense. She came out of the kitchen to see what was wrong. People stepped back to either side and she was staring straight at Mr. Bob. She was about to cut loose on him when he reached back and took Riches' lease from Doc. Riches tipped front and center. Mr. Bob said sweetly, "Now, Juliana, you can't banish a man bearing a dog."

Riches looked until he saw Jubal, who always followed Aunt Juliana about as if he were a dog. Then Riches haunched, stared at Jubal, and grinned. Mr. Bob reached down and removed his leash.

Aunt Juliana sensed that Jubal was the object of Riches' attention. As she turned towards the cat, Mr. Bob spoke quietly, "Seek Riches!"

Riches streaked. He flashed through Aunt Juliana's legs, nearly upsetting her, and then behind Jubal, and was laying something at Mr. Bob's feet before most of us realized what had happened. There came this gigantic M-I-A-OW-W-W-W-W," like a puma in an old MGM movie. Before Aunt Juliana had grasped that Jubal had found his voice, much less why, Doc went to tend him.

"There came this gigantic M-I-A-OW-W-W-W-W..."

As Mr. Bob was heading for Aunt Juliana, he thrust a fuzziness at me, whispering, "Whatever happens, keep this safe!" I looked down to see one of Jubal's tails.

Then Mr. Bob was saying loudly, "Juliana, you promised, 'The day Jubal talks is the day I sit down with Robert Hargrove!' By these witnesses, that time is here. I hereby request to exchange 'sit down' for 'marry with.'" People and animals went wild. TV cameras rolling. Suddenly Jubal jumped in Aunt Juliana's arms, his remaining tail waving proudly, his bandaged stub trying to keep pace. He was looking up at her and licking her face between mews.

Uncle Bob gave his bride a wiglet of tail hair to cover Jubal's stump on special occasions.

Aunt Juliana confided to mother that they had to lock Jubal out of the "nuptial chamber" because he wouldn't shut up. He pranced about telling anybody who would listen about his new-found grace. Mr. Bob confided to papa, "If that damn cat gets too cocky, I'll sic Riches on his other tail. I'm not called "Bob" for nothing!" Anyhow, Riches retained his name.

"...off to my grandparent's farm the day that I get out of school."

A TEENAGER'S LAMENT

K. PARKER STOOPS

I can't believe that they'd do this to me,
My parents are ever so cruel,
to send me right off to my grandparent's farm
the day that I get out of school.
"Have fun," they said—I'm like, "Oh, sure!"
'cause out here there's just nothing to do.
Today we went up to the lake and caught fish
And bailed out the boat with my shoe.

I can't believe how bizarre grandpa looks,
in his red flannel shirt and his beard,
when he sits after super and takes out his teeth
and the noise he makes—how weird!
The old John Deere tractor is parked in the barn
and grandpa says I get to drive,
"Turn left at the fencepost and go check the mail,
but keep her below fifty-five."

I can't believe all the ice cream I ate
at the Checkerboard Three-scoop Cafe.
Gail, the waitress, served extra French fries
And I met an old cowboy named Ray.
Delton P. Hubbard lives down cross the creek
On a ten-acre parcel of land.
His milk-cow, old Bossy, has just had a calf
and she licked up some corn from my hand.

I can't believe that the cat chased the dog
'round the yard until he chased her,
but at night they're together curled up by the fire,
in a warm-whiskered bundle of fur.
Grandma makes cookies each Monday at noon,
And when we get home around four
There's a tall glass of milk and a plate piled high,
"If you eat 'em, I'll have to make more!"

I can't believe that it's been three whole weeks,
but tomorrow I'm headed for home
back to TV and my poster-filled room,
my friends and my cellular phone.
Just as I thought, I've had no fun at all,
Been miserable day after day,
and the worst thing about it, from my point of view?
I was hopin' they'd ask me to stay.

PRETEND SHEPHERDS NEED REAL SHEEP

K. PARKER STOOPS

The year Pat Spartell was eleven, the Damp Flats Second Unilateral Church (and Social Organization) had a very memorable Christmas, indeed. For some time afterward, many of the parishioners thought that he and Jeffy Finkham had knocked Mrs. Gatacre's wig into the punchbowl on purpose.

Not surprisingly, Mrs.Gatacre herself was sometimes heard to say as much, when a few cups of punch had sufficiently loosened her tongue. That pair of stoics have borne the disgrace of that incident in silence for many years, thinking that it was better to let sleeping dogs lie, which they heartily wished to have done in the first place. But Pat never came back from his first tour in Vietnam, and Jeffy ran off and married that circus gal in California, and I'm thinking that before I pass on over the river Jordan, the record ought to be set straight. I saw the whole thing, and I tell you for a cast iron fact, the story started up with charity rather than greed. It happened like this.

The church, seen from the road, was an imposing structure. Perched on a small hill, it commanded a view of the whole town from the double front doors. On Sunday, the bell summoned believers from miles around, and they mounted the whitewashed steps to fill the scarred wooden pews and hear the Rev. Thockwiler espouse the virtues of reverence and clean living. The Christmas program of '61 was shaping up to be a really big show, largely due to the efforts of Mildred Eileen Gatacre.

Mrs. Gatacre was a stolid matron of the church, perhaps the foremost of the matrons. Her stolidity was unencumbered by the stabilizing influence of a husband, Mr. Gatacre having passed away ten years earlier. Her red face always exhibited a rather strained expression, possibly because of the concentration required to balance her massive pillar of blue-black hair that resembled the leaning tower of Pisa, only smaller. One time when debating a nuance of Unilateral theology with Spud Spotnick's father, a deacon, she lost her composure and told him off. I wasn't there, but Spud said it was something to see, spit running out the corner of her mouth and that pillar of hair doing the jitterbug, in defiance of the law of gravity. Fortunately, she was yelling loud enough to cover the sound of Spud busting out in laughter. His dad suddenly remembered some pressing business elsewhere, and took his leave before he busted out laughing, too.

Anyway, the nativity scene was going to be the highlight of the evening because Pat and Jeffy were tapped as shepherds, and they were determined to be the rootin' tootin'est shepherds that ever roped a sheep. Well, actually, those boys didn't have a sheep. What they had was Jeffy's dog Rex, wrapped in an old lace tablecloth and some silly-looking sheep ears strapped to his head. They could have had real sheep, if anybody knew where to find some, and if Mrs. Gatacre had allowed it, but she issued the decree in no uncertain terms that real sheep were dirty and smelly and only over her dead body would they be allowed inside the church, of all places. All of us fifth grade boys could see the sense of that.

Perhaps the sheep could walk past her body instead of over it, but Jeffy's mom scolded us for even thinking of the opportunity. So Rex endured a bath with store-bought soap and was locked out in the tractor shed overnight with the coal-oil heater going full blast. But at least the lads got to carry sticks (Mrs. Gatacre called them staffs, but everybody knew they were just sticks). A good stick comes in handy when a couple of young first time shepherds are herding their dog, minding their own business, and are suddenly accosted by a trio of sixth grade angels.

"We are the heavenly host! Don't be afraid."

So who's afraid? We have sticks, you've got halos.

"We bring good news! You must go to Bethlehem and see the King."

"You mean Elvis is playing in Bethlehem? And we didn't get tickets?"

"Unto you is born this day a Savior! Go and worship him!"

"Well, okay, but can we bring our dog? We can't just leave him here in the fields with these ears stuck on his head.

"Quit fooling around, you guys, and get to Bethlehem!"

"All right, all right. C'mon, Rex. Which way is Bethlehem, anyhow?"

After the nativity scene, the next best part of the program was the potluck dinner, and after that the 26-foot Christmas tree. Under Mrs. Gatacre's able direction, the high school boys had cut a silver fir out in Jack Ferris' woodlot and dragged it through the snow to the back church door, because the front door was locked and no one knew where the Rev. Thockwiler was. Eventually, they had to cut off about half the limbs to get it inside.

Unfortunately, they cut them all off the same side, but that made the tree easier to decorate because it lay flat on the floor, and then they just stood it up and leaned it against the back wall. Mrs. Gatacre's brilliant idea was to hang the tree with 25 or 30 envelopes. They each contained a card with a festive greeting, except one lucky envelope that had a crisp new five dollar bill. The idea was that after the potluck, everyone would come back upstairs and all the children would line up by age and take their turns at reaching an envelope, using a long wooden pole with a wire hook at one end.

In the fifth grade, most fellows are a little young to comprehend the finer points of Unilateral theology, but we did grasp one great truth: giving to the poor. In fact, the whole town was poor, but we didn't know that. We figured when the scripture talked of the poor, it meant people like Nancy Hewport and her family. Nancy was a grade behind us, and her shoes and clothes were always kind of ragged and dirty. Everybody knew her dad was a no-good drunk, living in a little shack at the edge of town. Most days at lunchtime, when we sat around with our brown bags and traded apples for Twinkies, Nancy had no lunch and sometimes we'd pitch in a spare cookie or half a sandwich. Of course "the poor" meant Nancy – who else could it possibly be?

Neither Jeffy or Pat was sufficiently godly to give Nancy any of their Christmas stuff, but they decided it would be a good deed to find the five dollar envelope and stick it at the back of the tree. Then they'd tell Nancy which one it was. If she didn't believe it and chose a different one, then the five bucks would split fifty-fifty between them. The only problem was, the church was always locked up tight except when Mrs. Gatacre was there decorating. The intrepid pair considered breaking in, but it seemed kind of sacreligious and besides, they weren't sure they could pull it off without getting caught. It looked like the plan was down the tubes, until the Friday night rehearsal brought new hope to their tiny, scheming minds.

The shepherds had to wait at the back of the stage while Mary talked to the angel, and then Joseph talked to the angel, and they made their long journey to Bethlehem and finally settled in at the stable. As it happened, they were waiting right next to the Christmas tree behind a low cardboard wall painted to resemble a manger, and someone had foolishly left the long pole laying right there. Jeffy snuck back and looked, and sure enough, with the spotlight on Mary and Joseph, it was pitch dark in the fields where the shepherds lay keeping their dog by night.

So it was that they taped up Jeffy's flashlight until the smallest pinhole of light leaked out, and he concealed it in his shepherd's robes. Pat decided to start at the bottom and work his way up. As Mary discussed her family situation with the angel, he slipped an envelope off its branch and extended it to Jeffy, who flashed the pinhole ever so briefly, shook his head and grinned. Pat handed over three, then four more, and then he had to start using the pole. About ten envelopes later, just as the wise men found what they had been seeking, the boys found what they'd been seeking also and Jeffy stuffed the flashlight down his pants.

"Put it at the very top," he whispered. "'Way at the back, where nobody can see it." Reaching as high as he could, Pat twisted the packet onto a slender branch and got the pole stuck. He twisted and tugged, but it was bound up for good.

"Hurry up!" hissed Jeffy. "We have to tend our dog!"
"I can't get it loose! Get over here and give me a hand!"

And there were in the same country, shepherds in the field, watching their dogs by night. And just as the host of angels appeared in the sky, a shepherd stumbled backward over the dog, who yelped as a tall tree crashed down into the middle of the stable, and the sky was filled with light, and they were sore afraid. But behold, amid the snickers of the audience, Joseph and the three wise men helped the shepherds drag the tree out of the way, and the rest of the program proceeded without incident. More or less.

Until after the potluck dinner, where Mrs. Gatacre stood up in front and rapped her spoon on the punchbowl to get everyone's attention. "Ladies and gentlemen, I have some bad news to announce. The envelope picking will not take place this evening because two boys are suspected of stealing the five-dollar prize. I am truly disappointed in them and I know you will be also. At this time I would like them to stand up and return the..."

"…just as the host of angels appeared in the sky, a shepherd stumbled backward over the dog…"

Startled, she turned suddenly at the sound of a loud yelp from the side door, where Spud's father had accidentally stepped on Rex's tail. The centrifugal force was too much for the shimmering pillar of hair, which slowly slid to the side and toppled off her head, landing in the punchbowl.

In the split second before the room erupted in laughter, I remember thinking, "She's got gray whiskers on her head! Just like Grandpa's face when he doesn't shave for a few days." After that, the memories kind of blur together.

Jeffy and Pat chased Rex around for quite a while, bumping into people with Mrs. Gatacre shrieking, "Get that animal outside! Out, do you hear me? This is a disgrace to the house of God!" By the time they finally caught him, the sheep ears were history, the lace tablecloth was in ragged tatters, and Mrs. Gatacre had squeezed most of the punch out of her soggy wig and put the wreckage back on her head. After the boys locked Rex in the trunk of Mr. Finkham's old Pontiac and took all the tape off Jeffy's flashlight, there was about nothing left to do but head on for home.

Two days later, Mr. Spotnick dragged the Christmas tree out the front doors and around behind the shed, where he lit it on fire. It was probably just a coincidence, but Nancy showed up at school the next week with a brand-new pair of shoes. Said her mom found some money on their porch Christmas Eve.

"Was it five bucks in a white envelope, Nancy? Real crisp and new?" Pat asked the question quietly, and then his eyes slowly widened.

"I think so. Hey, how do you know that?"

"No reason, just a lucky guess. Here, take this half a sandwich off my hands, wouldja? I'm not real hungry today."

"...the centrifugal force was too much for the shimmering pillar of hair..."

"The sparks sure fly in Texas, when the devil stomps his feet..."

THE LEGEND OF BANJO PICKIN' JAKE

K. PARKER STOOPS

Late one August Friday night
the devil came to town
to the Brazos Arms Cantina,
where the cowboys hang around.
He strutted through the swingin' door
and pushed up to the bar.
As quick as a wink he was holdin' a drink
and starin' at the steel guitar.

He walked out on the dance floor
and turned to face the band.
"I hear it round you're the best in town
and known throughout the land.
I sure do feel like scootin' a boot
'til early mornin' light.
Perhaps you'd care to take a dare
and hoedown me tonight."

It's Friday night in Texas
and the Devil's here to dance,
but many a man has lost his soul
by takin' a reckless chance.
Don't do nuthin' stupid, son,
you'll make a big mistake.
Learn a lesson from the tale
of Banjo Pickin' Jake.

Them pickers all turned ghostly white
and scattered east and west.
Dove up and down and sideways,
gettin' clear of that request.
The devil gave a chuckle
'cause he'd put 'em on the run.
Just like a pack of scalded dogs,
they all lit out-'cept one.

Ol' Jake, the banjo picker,
was a little short on cash.
He'd set a spell in the blue motel
eatin' day-old beans and hash.
He grunted at the devil,
"Hey, I don't pick for free,
the crack of dawn's a long way off,
what's in the deal for me?"

It's Friday night in Texas
and Jake is talkin' bold,
but the devil'd like to own his soul
before he knows it's sold.
Don't do nuthin' stupid, son,
too big a chance to take.
Nuthin good can come of this,
Banjo Pickin' Jake.

The devil smiled an evil smile
and spoke real soft and sweet.
"I've got a special somethin',
that'll skip your heart a beat."
A shiny golden banjo,
I'll offer you to bet.
The kind that any pickin' man
would sell his soul to get."

Jake said, "Does this here Banjo
have a diamond studded strap?
Does each and every tunin' peg
have a ruby on its cap?"
The devil said, "You betcha,
if that's what you desire;
Whatever it takes to make a deal
to drown your soul in fire!"

The devil's down here in Texas,
and he's givin' away the store,
and poor old Jake's been suckered in
like many a man before.
He traded off his mortal soul
for a cruise on Devil's Lake
where the fiery waves will slowly swallow
Banjo Pickin' Jake.

Then a fiddler name of Johnny
said, "Jake, I'm cuttin' in.
I like your style and I'll crawl a mile,
'fore I'll see the Devil win.
Once I lived in Georgia
and he showed up down there, too.
I whupped him then and we can whup him now,
and I'm proud to fiddle with you."

Smoke poured out the devil's ears
and he hollered, "That ain't fair!"
But Johnny just turned the devil an eye
and pulled him up a chair.
He tightened up his fiddle strings
and Jake said,"Here we go!"
Then they swung into the classic
known to all as Cotton-eyed Joe.

The sparks sure fly in Texas
when the devil stomps his feet,
and you'd better keep him dancin'
to an old-time country beat.
Once you start the music playin',
don't slow down, for Heaven's sake.
Your only choice is to move them fingers,
Banjo Pickin' Jake.

Well, you all know the story,
how them two played all night,
and just when they were plumb played out,
there come the mornin' light.
A beaming ray of sunshine
was a thing the devil feared,
and with a flash and cloud of smoke,
he up and disappeared.

But right where he had last been seen
a golden banjo lay.
Jake rubbed his eyes in stunned surprise
that there wasn't Hell to pay.
But when he went and picked it up,
well, that was all she wrote,
'cause that flashy golden banjo
wouldn't play a single note.

That's how it is in Texas,
when the devil comes around.
The banjo you end up with,
though it's gold, don't make a sound.
Those strings don't pick for nothin',
it's a phony and a fake.
You musta been bamboozled,
Banjo Pickin' Jake.

Banjo on his shoulder,
Jake strolled across the town.
He walked up to the foundry,
said, "melt this sucker down."
I guess you heard the Devil
made me look like some buffoon.
Now, I want you boys to work me up
a diamond-edged spittoon. "

When the foundrymen had finished,
his walk back was twice as far,
cause he had to brag and show it off
on his way back to the bar.
The last time that I saw him
was beside the old dance floor,
just a-spittin' his tobacco
in that golden cuspidor.

If you're gonna play in Texas
and you're gonna make a deal
with a curly-tailed devil
afire your soul to steal,
hold out for the go-round, pard,
there's some comfort you might take
from the legend of the gold spittoon
and Banjo Pickin' Jake.

THE HOUSEGUESTS

GREG TULEJA

When Sean and Elaine Mitchell moved from Philadelphia to Jaffrey, New Hampshire, they felt prepared to make the transition from their energetic urban lifestyle to the humdrum habits and routines of life in the country. They were ready to give up the whimsical midnight excursions for pizza and ice cream, Saturday afternoons at Wanamakers, and all the greasy cheese steaks they could eat. They admitted that they would miss the pulse and the variety of the city, but not the crime, the litter, or the nightly squawking of the neighborhood hookers, gathered on the corner beneath their apartment window, searching aggressively for eager clients with available cash. Eight years in Philadelphia had been fun, but city life had become tiring, and after a year of long distance house hunting and five scouting trips to New England, they found a house in New Hampshire. They were seeking peace and quiet, and with the 1796 Colonial on three acres of ground, they believed that they had found it.

Their first spring and summer were just what they expected. They enjoyed the crisp starlit nights, the singing of the spring peepers in May, fresh vegetables from their own garden and sitting outdoors far into the night without a sound of a hooker anywhere. They soon fell in step with the more relaxed pace of country life, and it became rare for them to complain about the lack of fresh bagels or the absence of an art gallery within walking distance. If not for the events that occurred on the property during their first autumn in the house, Sean and Elaine might very well have become completely adapted to their new life as transplanted New Englanders, and they might still be there now, listening to the loons and to the owls, rocking themselves into middle age on the front porch. However, the unexpected did play its part. Although the events themselves were not record-breaking, and by the standards of the native country folk of New Hampshire not even unusual, to the Mitchells the whole affair had an exotic taste that was a touch too strong. They emerged physically unscathed, but their enthusiasm was dampened, and their resolve to embrace the spirit of rural America was permanently weakened.

It all started one evening in early October. While the Mitchells were relaxing after dinner, Elaine heard a light scratching sound from the roof of the family room. At first she took little notice of the noise – odd sounds in the old house were frequent. She was used to pinecones falling on the roof or windows rattling in the wind. She thought that it was probably something like that. But when she heard it again, this time much louder, Elaine realized it was not the wind. Like all noises made by wild animals, the sound lacked a certain pattern and regularity, and it was clear to her that there was a brain directing those scratching noises, perhaps a primitive one, but with a motive.

"Do you hear that, Sean?" asked Elaine.
"Yes, I hear it. It sounds like something crawling on the roof."

"Maybe it's a bird or a mouse," said Elaine hopefully. The noise soon stopped and the Mitchells forgot about it until the next evening when they again heard scratching and scuffling. This time it sounded as if it were going up one side of the house, over the roof, and down the wall on the other side.

They both went outside with flashlights but saw nothing. Back inside the family room, the noise had mysteriously stopped, and they went to bed with faint stirrings of alarm. That night Sean dreamed that there were dozens of mice and birds and giant shrews scrambling all over the roof and the walls of the house, chattering to one another in some secret, bestial code. He awoke trembling. He was surprised not to see Elaine next to him but heard her calling him from the next room.

"Sean! Come in here! Listen to this!"

She was crouching on the floor with her head up against the wall. Sean knelt beside her. The now familiar scratching sound was distinct, and this time they also detected a faint murmuring.

Sean whispered, "Is that...purring?" Elaine shook her head. "It's nibbling, Sean." There was no doubt – some kind of animal was having a meal on the other side of the wall. They both reached the obvious conclusion that whatever it was, it was inside the house.

Sean offered what he knew was an unlikely explanation. "It's probably a mouse."

Elaine replied generously, "Yes, probably a mouse." This was said without enthusiasm, since both Sean and Elaine, in spite of their decidedly tenderfoot status as naturalists, could tell quite clearly that it sounded quite a bit larger than a mouse.

On the way home from work the next day, they stopped at the hardware store in Jaffrey and bought some traps. They set some in the attic and in the basement, and the next morning they were pleased to find two mice caught. Over the next few days, as the count rose to five, the Mitchells felt that they were dealing with the small-scale infestation with true backcountry know-how, developed steadily over six whole months of living in New Hampshire.

On the third morning, these contests took on a new character. Checking a trap in the attic, Sean found it sprung, with just a paw and foreleg pinned securely by the metal bar of the trap. The the mouse's leg was a sickening sight. The mouse had probably bled to died somewhere, but it had succeeded in cheating its enemies out of the victory of claiming the dead body. This act of determination by the tiny animal impressed Sean, and for the first time, he recognized these confrontations between man and beast, not as household duties, like cleaning the gutters or sweeping the stairs, but as a life and death struggle. To the mice, this invasion, if that is what it was, was filled with deadly risks and the trap was a hideous reminder if the seriousness of the situation from the mouse's point of view.

That night the Mitchells went out to dinner, and returning home from the restaurant, they had forgotten about their problems with the local rodents. Suddenly, the headlights fell on a moving object on the ground next to the house. Sean stopped the car and they both stared ahead. Standing proudly on its hind legs, gazing back at them as if to challenge their arrival, extended to full height and greedily illuminated by the headlights like an operatic tenor stepping forward for one final encore, was a red squirrel.

Sean was temporarily paralyzed, but Elaine took action. She stepped out of the car and slammed the door. Taking a few steps forward, Elaine waved her arms, stamped her feet and shouted threats at the startled squirrel which abruptly retreated. This initial confrontation appeared to be a clear victory for Elaine, but the squirrel was then seen to vanish behind the lowest clapboard of the family room wall. They approached the house. Fearfully reaching under the clapboard, Sean felt around with his fingers at the precise location where the squirrel had disappeared. It was definitely a hole, certainly big enough for a squirrel to squeeze through. The edges were chipped and splintered where the hole had been expanded into an adequate entrance by the powerful incisors of the squirrel, which was now certainly in the house. The Mitchells did not sleep well that night.

The next morning they discussed strategy. "Maybe we could just plug up the hole when we see it outside somewhere," suggested Elaine.

"We could do that. But there might be more than one, and we wouldn't want to trap any inside," said Sean.

"More than one?" Elaine pondered this distasteful possibility, her voice taking on a new edge.

"Elaine, we'll have to kill it. Or them. But don't worry, rattraps are very powerful. It won't suffer."

'Elaine replied, "Mary Stuart wasn't expecting to suffer either, and look what happened to her. They say she survived three strokes of the ax."

Sean and Elaine smiled sadly at each other. They truly regretted that a poor little squirrel, searching instinctively for adequate shelter for the coming winter, hopelessly overwhelmed by the size and intellect of its human opponents, would have to die. However, they had their pride to consider. They were determined to defeat the squirrel.

Mishandling the rattraps could mean much more than just a sore finger, so Sean and Elaine were very careful as they set them in the basement, delicately baiting them with bits of cheese. They tested each one by poking it with a long wooden dowel, which was cleanly, furiously snapped off as the metal bar was released. To place one in the attic, Sean had to crawl through a low door, carrying a flashlight deep under the eaves. As he tiptoed back down the attic stairs, he thought of the fully loaded rattrap, sitting ominously in the dark corner, waiting. Before going to sleep that night, Elaine said, "So what do we do now, just wait here for the screams of agony?"

"Don't worry, we won't hear anything from here. We'll just check them in the morning."

After climbing the attic steps at 6 a.m., Sean opened the door, poked his head in, and shined his flashlight under the eaves. There it was! A red squirrel was lying lifeless in the trap. Pleased with their success in defending the family territory, Sean yelled down to Elaine, We got him!" Congratulating each other, they inspected the squirrel.

Elaine said, "Now, let's plug up that hole."

But Sean was cautious. "Let's wait a few more days." Smiling, he added with mock horror, "There may be dozens more."

"Sean, if there are dozens, I'll just rent a house on the beach, and you can call me when it's over."

For three uneventful days, there were no scratching or chomping sounds coming from inside the walls of the Mitchell's house, and no new victims found in the traps. Sean and Elaine felt confident that they were again in sole possession of their home, and they planned to collect the traps the next morning. As they fell off to sleep, they were satisfied with their resourcefulness.

At 3 a.m., they were both awakened by the sound. It was a high-pitched squealing noise, coming from the attic, a screeching and clattering sound of wood knocking against wood.

"What the hell is that?" gasped Sean.

"Well, Sean, I'll go out on a limb on this one. My guess is that there is small rodent upstairs caught in a trap. Let me know if you need any help."

"Thanks, Elaine, thanks a lot."

As Sean slowly climbed the attic steps, he could imagine what was happening behind the door in that dark and dusty corner beneath the roof, but actually seeing it, in the full glare of the flashlight, was a terrible shock. There in front of him, not two feet away, was a second red squirrel, wailing pitifully. It had been caught in the trap, and in a desperate and futile attempt to escape, it was thrashing the trap from side to side, dragging it around the floor. This whole episode had begun to take on an aspect they hadn't anticipated. He knew that he would have to kill it.

Although disabled, the squirrel seemed to have quite enough energy to bite him on the nose or thumb, and Sean thought for a moment that the job would ideally be accomplished from a distance. He considered various methods of doing away with the squirrel and rejected each of them; Some were impractical, some too ghoulish. He evaluated various elaborate methods of electrocution, and he pictured himself pulling the final switch from some remote room in the house so that he would not have to witness the execution. But this creative and irrational reverie lasted only a few moments. Sean soon snapped back to reality.

He ran downstairs, grabbed a hammer and returned to the attic. Crawling back into the darkness under the roof, he could see that the squirrel had been trying to back down a small space in the floorboards, but the trap, still firmly attached, kept getting caught. It had stopped struggling and sat motionless, staring at Sean. As he raised the hammer, the squirrel blinked and whimpered softly, and Sean could see its heart beating wildly. Sweating and trembling, he took a deep breath. He did not want to be in that position and wanted to be anywhere but where he was. He slowly lowered the hammer, repositioned himself slightly, and raised it again. The squirrel looked up at him. Sean was surprised at the difficulty he was having and he somehow seized upon a countdown as a solution. Loud enough for the squirrel to hear, but entirely for his own benefit, Sean counted, "ONE, TWO, THREE!" The hammer still did not move. Sean sat back heavily and whispered to the squirrel, "Don't look at me! I won't be able to do this if you look at me." The squirrel started clattering around with the trap again.

Sean ran down to the kitchen and got some paper grocery bags and returned to the attic. Elaine was sitting on the edge of the bed, listening, apparently ready to help, but happy not to be involved unless it was absolutely necessary.

As Sean thundered up the stairs, sprinting past the bedroom door, she asked, "How's it going? Do you need any help?"

Sean replied breathlessly, "I'm getting there."

Back in the attic, Sean propped up the flashlight, inserted one paper bag inside another and placed it on the floor next to the squirrel, which was looking slightly away from him. He picked up the trap and dropped it, and the the squirrel, into the paper bags. As Sean rolled the top of the bag closed, the squirrel started thrashing around and squealing. Bounding down the stairs, Sean looked like a shopper in a great hurry to return home from the mall with a very unusual purchase. He ran outside to the patio and set the bag down. Out in the open, Sean's resolve was firmer, and this time there was no need to count.

Elaine joined him outside, and together they performed a short, somber ceremony in the woods behind the house. The white light of the rising moon, their whispered words of apology forming small clouds of silver vapor in the cool autumn air, they buried the squirrel. Elaine placed a heavy stone over the grave and that was the end of the squirrel problem at the Mitchell's house.

Sean and Elaine continued to live in Jaffrey for another year, experiencing other less spectacular engagements with the local wildlife, but they never fully recovered from the trauma caused by their uninvited houseguests. The Mitchells eventually moved back to Philadelphia, where the ecological balance between humans and wild animals was not so delicate, and the boundary between wilderness and civilization not quite so blurred. They resumed their late night trips to the neighborhood deli and began a subscription to the ballet. The hookers on the corner were still busy and noisy, as much a part of the natural landscape of Philadelphia as were the squirrels back in New Hampshire, but at least they did not try to come into the apartment. Back in the city, the Mitchells were only rarely forced to confront nature in its pure state. Once they heard a mouse rummaging around under the sink, but their solution was much simpler, if less direct, than it had been back in Jaffrey.

"Back in the city, the Mitchells were only rarely forced to confront nature in its pure state."

They made a phone call to the super.